JESS,
CHUNK,
AND THE
ROAD TRIP
TO
INFINITY

JESS, CHUNK, and the

ROAD TRIP to INFINITY

Kristin Elizabeth Clark

Farrar Straus Giroux · New York

Farrar Straus Giroux Books for Young Readers
An imprint of Macmillan Publishing Group, LLC
175 Fifth Avenue, New York 10010

Text copyright © 2016 by Kristin Elizabeth Clark
All rights reserved
Printed in the United States of America
Designed by Elizabeth H. Clark
First edition, 2016

1   3   5   7   9   10   8   6   4   2

fiercereads.com

Library of Congress Cataloging-in-Publication Data

Names: Clark, Kristin Elizabeth, author.
Title: Jess, Chunk, and the road trip to infinity / Kristin Elizabeth Clark.
Description: First edition. | New York : Farrar Straus Giroux, 2016. |
    Summary: "A male-to-female trans teen, Jess, and her male best friend,
    Chunk, take a road trip across the country to attend Jess's father's wedding to
    her mother's former best friend"—Provided by publisher.
Identifiers: LCCN 2015039501 | ISBN 9780374380069 (hardcover : alk. paper) |
    ISBN 9780374380076 (e-book)
Subjects: | CYAC: Transgender people—Fiction. | Automobile travel—Fiction. |
    Best friends—Fiction. | Friendship—Fiction. | Fathers and sons—Fiction. |
    Mothers and daughters—Fiction. | BISAC: JUVENILE FICTION /
    Social Issues / Friendship.
Classification: LCC PZ7.C54827 Je 2016 | DDC [Fic]—dc23
LC record available at https://lccn.loc.gov/2015039501

Our books may be purchased in bulk for promotional, educational, or business use.
Please contact your local bookseller or the Macmillan Corporate and Premium
Sales Department at (800) 221-7945 ext. 5442 or by e-mail
at MacmillanSpecialMarkets@macmillan.com.

With deep gratitude, this book is dedicated to its doula, Joy Peskin.
Thank you for helping these two crazy kids breathe their first.
You are an extraordinary editor and a kickass human being.

JESS, CHUNK, AND THE ROAD TRIP TO INFINITY

AUTHOR'S NOTE

In the past few years, a lot has changed in terms of visibility around matters of gender identity and expression. Certainly there are more trans stories being published and talked about than there used to be.

This thrills me both as an ally, and as a mother who loves her child deeply.

My daughter was held up at birth and erroneously pronounced male. Many years later, when she was a young adult, she let me know her truth—an act of bravery that changed us both for the good.

When she came out to me as trans, one of the first emotions I felt was fear *for* her, though I tried not to let her see it. As a longtime supporter of the LGBTQIA community, I was well aware of how brutal the world could be to individuals who didn't fall into narrow hetero- and cis-normative categories. And even now, these many years later, every time I learn of a hate crime against anyone queer, but especially against someone who is trans, I think of my own child.

Every. Single. Time.

I know I can't lead my beautiful daughter around by the hand shouting, "Hey, world! Don't hurt her!" All I can do is try to make the world a better, less dangerous place, by giving other people a sense of what it might be like to walk in the shoes of someone who's trans.

My daughter and other trans individuals I've met were inspiration for both *Jess, Chunk, and the Road Trip to Infinity*, and my earlier novel, *Freakboy* (also featuring gender queer characters). The books themselves, though, are works of fiction, and any resemblance the characters may have to anyone, living or not, is entirely coincidental.

It's my fervent hope that my books (and books like them) can lead us all to a greater understanding and acceptance of gender's vast and lovely variations.

All best,
Kristin Elizabeth Clark

CHAPTER 1

Something about my mom's New Age music makes me want to stab myself in the eye. Although anatomically speaking, the ear might be a better area to stab if I'm serious about not having to listen to it anymore. The sound is coming from the living room and our house is so small there's no escaping it.

I'm in my bedroom packing to the backdrop of a thrumming harp and the low hollow shriek of a bamboo flute. Underneath that there's the *shhhhht* of the *Vogue* magazine sliding into my laptop case, and the *snick* of a Viva La Juicy perfume bottle hitting my straight-edge razor. It's five days after high school graduation, I'm packing for my first parent-free road trip, and I can almost hear my old life and my new one clinking against each other.

I add a couple of button-down shirts and some girl jeans to the Space Camp duffel bag I've had since seventh grade.

I'm definitely going to need new luggage before I head off to college in August.

Wallet, check.

Sweatshirt, check.

Sketchbook, check.

Mom comes in and hands me a tube of sunscreen.

"I have some." I open my bag a little wider so she can see.

"That's only SPF fifty," she says. "This is seventy."

I sigh and take the seventy.

"No skin cancer for you!" she says in a weird accent. I know it's a reference to some comedy skit about soup or something, but I'm damned if I know what's funny about it.

"Just want you to be safe," she says in her normal voice. Her urge to protect me can be irritating, but just now I'm heading halfway across the country—San Jose to Chicago without her—and in this case her concern might be warranted.

I look at her and smile.

Her hair used to be straight like mine, but five years ago she had cancer, and after remission her hair grew back soft and wavy. She calls it the chemo curl.

Even with different hair, people say we look a lot alike. Same blue eyes, same noses, and now that I'm taking hormones, I swear our jawlines are becoming similar too.

It's not that I want us to dress in matching outfits or anything, but when you're transitioning, there are worse things than realizing you look like your mom. Especially if your mom is as beautiful as mine used to be.

"You're wearing that?" she asks, indicating the thin white Power Puff Girls T-shirt I slept in last night. Earlier than expected results from hormones are in evidence. (Yay, breasts!)

I point to a thicker T-shirt and the light blue hoodie lying on my bed.

I've been taking hormones for seven months now, since November 22, the day I turned eighteen, and I'm kind of at an in-between-looking place at this point.

People who know me see what they expect to see, what they think they've seen all along. A sort of skinny guy with a shortish body and longish hair. But under a thin shirt it's obvious that breasts are growing.

I'm friendly with a few kids from my art classes and theater, but I'm not tight with any of them, so my mom and my best friend Chunk are the only ones who (privately) use the right pronouns and call me by my new name (Jess). They're also the only ones who know about my (I'm gonna go ahead and say it) new development.

I toss a pair of nondescript jeans on top of the thick T-shirt and hoodie mix on the bed. Mom nods, satisfied that I'm not putting myself in danger by flaunting my sexy lady body at a time when rigorous shaving is still necessary, and turns to leave. "Breakfast in five."

The clock says 8:30.

"I need to finish packing so we can get on the road!"

"You're in a hurry for someone who originally didn't want to go," she says over her shoulder.

I'm an expert at decoding my mom's voice; her tone is singsongy, teasing, and not malicious at all.

"You're right," I agree.

I haven't spoken to my dad in more than a year, since he'd refused to cosign a waiver that would have allowed me to get hormones before I was eighteen. The fact that it ultimately worked out okay in terms of timing—I was graduating high school identifying as a boy and starting college identifying as a girl—didn't make me any less bitter about having my gender dysphoria dismissed as a phase.

Six weeks ago, when the invitation to his wedding showed up, my mom opened it. ("I wanted to see if it was what I thought it was, so we could talk about it" was her excuse for invading my privacy.)

I said no effing way am I going. In fact, before dropping the RSVP card in the mail, I practically scratched a hole in the paper over the box marked *Regrets* and then wrote the word *no* over it, just to make sure my father and his cow of a fiancée got my point.

I'm not going to your wedding and I'm not sorry.

Bizarrely enough, my mom thought I should go.

"Anger is a coal that burns only the person who holds it," she told me.

She's been a lunatic all my life in one way or another. Currently she's a very peaceful and New Agey one. A year and a half ago she went to a retreat for cancer survivors and came back saying things like "In Spiritual Forgiveness, there are no victims. Everything is in Divine Order," and "All is in accordance with our soul contracts."

Pretty impressive for someone whose EX-HUSBAND IS MARRYING HER FORMER BEST FRIEND.

Except for the (to me) interminable year Jan lived with her boyfriend Roger, my mom's best friend, single and childless, spent so much time at our house we called the guest room Jan's Lair. She and I hung out a ton. She bought me a sketchbook for my eighth birthday and then made Saturday morning art lessons a tradition. She'd drive me up to Big Basin State Park, just so I could sketch the redwoods because they were my favorite things to draw.

That's right. My father the transphobe is marrying a woman I called Aunt Jan for most of my life.

And my mother's "Spiritual Acceptance" is taking some getting used to.

Because really, when you've settled into a groove of hating your father it's nicer to have someone hating him right alongside you, you know?

In any case, it wasn't Mom who convinced me to travel the two thousand miles to the wedding.

It was Chunk.

- - - - - - -

"Don't forget you'll need to clean the kitchen before you leave," Mom calls from down the hall.

Some things are non-negotiable. My cleaning the kitchen after meals is one of them. According to her (recent) philosophy, when your kitchen is in the fêng shui health area of your house, tidiness is of the utmost importance.

"Then you're going to have to change the music," I call back, and turn to my closet. Next to a pair of skinny jeans, on the side of the closet I think of as the girl side, hangs the costume I designed for the character of Muzzy when our school did *Thoroughly Modern Millie* a couple of months ago.

The girl who played Muzzy and I happen to be a similar size. And it also happens that I designed a glorious garment that *somehow* fits me to a T.

Imagine that.

Besides the Muzzy dress and the skinny jeans, there are only a couple of outfits on the girl side of the closet. Two shirts with intricate designs and flowy, floaty hems and sleeves, plus a pair of wide-legged yoga pants that I got at East West, my mom's favorite hippie store.

I've only ever worn the shirts and yoga pants inside my house.

The clothes I wear in public are pretty gender-neutral: sweatshirts, boy jeans, a few button-down shirts, run-of-the-mill hoodies, paint-splattered Vans. So far, mine is a no-style style. It's kind of boring, but designed to fly under the radar. Important at Kennedy High, but not anymore.

I shiver.

There's no way the Muzzy dress will fly under any radar. It weighs a ton because the entire thing is covered in black sequins, except for the bodice, which is slashed across the front with silver bugle beads. The cut is long and narrow, with a slit up the side.

I've never shown my true self to the outside world, and yet this is what I plan to wear to my father's wedding.

Because, really, nothing says "F U, Dad" like showing up

in a dress, when he used to make you wear a Cub Scout uniform.

I take the sublime, sequined concoction off the hanger and gently roll it around a pair of black satin ballet flats. My hand fumbles with the zipper when I close the duffel bag.

Am I really going to do this?

- - - - - -

During breakfast we have the wear-your-seat-belt-and-sunscreen-and-be-careful-of-strangers-and-check-in-once-a-day-unless-you-want-me-to-put-out-an-APB-on-you-and-I'm-very-proud-of-you-for-going conversation. Then Mom goes off to get dressed for work while I do the dishes.

Really, I don't know how she's going to survive the next week without having me around to be all concerned about.

I've just put soap in the dishwasher and closed the door when she comes back in wearing the nurse's scrubs that have little yellow ducks sporting handlebar mustaches. She says the kids on the pediatric ward love them.

We made several sets of scrubs for her during our sewing-together phase. We've also had a gardening-together phase (which I hated), and a knitting-together phase. I drew the line when she wanted us to have a taking-dance-classes-together phase.

"What time is Chuck picking you up?" she asks.

"I told him I'd walk to his house and we'd leave from there."

If I waited for Chunk to come get me, we might never get this show on the road. I love the guy, but he takes his own sweet time in doing just about everything.

"Grab your things. I'll give you a ride," she says, keys in hand.

I think about it for a second and shake my head.

"I have a little more stuff I need to do here."

The truth is, I want to take the first few steps of this trip on my own, but I know if I try explaining that, it'll sound like I'm making the whole thing overly momentous or something.

Once we leave San Jose, I feel like I'll be free to be me, full time. Instead of he/his/him Jeremy Saunders, I'll finally be she/hers/her Jessica Saunders. Jess for short.

"I'll wait. I can be a bit late," she says.

"No. Thank you, though." I step in for a hug.

She holds on for a second longer than necessary and murmurs, "I'll miss you."

"I'll miss you too."

"I wish you'd let him know you're coming."

I step out of her hug. "My terms," I remind her.

When I changed my mind about going, I didn't get in touch with Dad and Jan to let them know. With the exception of the RSVP card, I haven't broken my no-Jess-initiated-contact record in nearly two years.

Not that silence on my part ever stopped my dad from trying to get in touch with me, but I delete all his e-mails without reading them, and on the top shelf of my closet there're a bunch of letters and cards from him I've never read.

"They don't get to think they can just summon me."

"Jess, that's not what . . . ," my mom starts to say.

"It's the only way I'm going."

And if I end up chickening out, no one but Chunk will be any the wiser.

- - - - - -

When she finally leaves for work, I go into my room and grab the unopened mail from my dad, plus the card with the location and time of the ceremony on it. I shove it all into my laptop case next to my computer and *Vogue*.

Even now, almost six weeks after deciding to do this, I don't have an actual plan for what I'm going to say, or even at what point during the wedding or reception I'm going to show up.

There's one thing I do know, though. If my dad says one assholic thing to me, my nonplan plan involves throwing every single envelope in his face and walking out.

I glance around my room to make sure I have everything. It's kind of hard to tell in the cramped chaos of my futon, my desk, my drafting table, and the easel sitting on a rumpled cloth tarp that's stiff with paint. Every surface is littered with X-Acto knives, sable brushes of varying thicknesses, vine charcoal, chalk, pigments, and various objets trouvés— the odds and ends I've collected to use in collages: scraps of newspaper, old postcards, and even dryer lint that has an interesting indigo color shot through with a gold thread. When my mom complains, I point to the hand-lettered sign on the huge bulletin board running the length of one wall: A CREATIVE MESS IS ALWAYS BETTER THAN A TIDY IDLENESS.

My gaze rests on the album of photos from my art school application—my portfolio. Between its padded gray covers are the scanned pictures of thirteen mixed-media self-portraits. (The fact that my work mainly consists of paintings of *me* really says something, huh?)

I'm still experimenting, finding my way as an artist, but the one thing my pieces all have in common is that each one was inspired by a specific memory. And every painting in my portfolio strongly features a particular color, so when viewed all together there's a whole rainbow thing going on.

My private joke with me.

The letter of acceptance from Stern used adjectives like *remarkable, gifted, raw,* and *evocative* to describe my art.

Six months later those words still give me warm goose bumps.

I can't imagine a scenario in which I'll be sitting around showing my portfolio to Dad and Jan, but I grab the album anyway. On the drafting table underneath it there's a photo of a piece inspired by a day I spent with Chunk not too long ago. The work is too recent to have been in my art school application, but it's one of my favorites. I tuck the picture loosely inside the front cover and slide the whole thing into my backpack.

It just fits.

— — — — — — —

Blue

10x14 inches

> Image: Ocean painted over roller coaster line drawing.
> Portrait of the artist in the front car. The artist's
> expression—mouth open, eyes wide—is one of
> simultaneous terror and delight. Tiny dresses, red
> foil alternating with blue, line the border.
> Acrylic, black ink on paper, foil

On Senior Beach Day, Kennedy High traditionally packs the graduating class into buses and sends them to the Santa Cruz Beach Boardwalk for a day of fun in the sun, hoping to stave off a true senior ditch day. The school reserves volleyball courts and provides wristbands for the rides. The ocean provides all the water you can swim in.

Not that there was even the most remote possibility of me or Chunk taking a dip.

He's a big guy. He wears huge tent-like shirts, and sometimes I notice him tugging the material away from his body.

It's a gesture familiar to me. Even wearing a sports bra underneath a heavy T-shirt and hoodie, when I was around people from school I hunched my shoulders to keep the material loose and off my frame.

Neither of us was willing to show the outline of our bodies to the world.

Chunk and I were convinced that ride maintenance was taken care of by toothless crack addicts, so we ditched the boardwalk with its smell of corn dogs and funnel cakes for the ocean scent of salt and tar. We walked along the shoreline, occasionally stopping to let the frigid waters of the Pacific break over our feet.

I do not love amusement parks, I do not love volleyball, I do not love the great outdoors, and I definitely do not love being surrounded by girls who were born with girl parts lolling around the beach in their bikinis.

I do, however, love hanging with Chunk.

Gulls shrieked in the distance, and we stopped to watch some boogie boarders. It had been two days since I'd received the wedding invitation, and I was ranting (again) about my dickhead dad, and his cow of a fiancée, Jan.

"I'm sure he doesn't even really want me there . . . He probably just invited me because it would look bad if he didn't invite his only offspring. I can't believe my mom thought I should go."

Chunk had been listening patiently like a friend is supposed to do, but then he disagreed with me, which a friend is not supposed to do.

"I think you should go," he said, foamy surf swirling around our ankles. "My mom says . . ."

"I know what your mom says," I snapped.

Dr. Georgia Kefala was all about me "repairing the relationship" with my dad.

Another wave crashed, and Chunk kept talking like he didn't hear me. "Besides, don't you want to show him who you are?"

"Black Hole," I practically shouted, which is code for *leave it alone.*

I turned away and stalked up the beach, leaving Chunk just standing in the water.

When Black Hole is invoked, we agree to drop whatever it is we've been talking about. If the other person brings up the dreaded subject that Black Hole has been called on, the person who called it gets to punch the offender in the arm.

Still, calling Black Hole didn't stop the words *Don't you want to show him who you are?* from echoing in my ear.

I pictured myself standing at the back of the church in a long red dress and kitten heels, and when the minister asked if anyone had any objections, I'd part my perfectly made-up lips to say "I do." There'd be shock on my dad's face, and murmurs of "Who's that girl?" I imagined him starting down the aisle to tell this young woman off for disrupting the wedding, but then he'd get closer and recognize me. That'd show him who I am, all right.

I'd just reached the softer, harder-to-stalk-through sand when Chunk came up behind me, throwing a strong arm around my shoulder. I almost fell but he steadied me, turning me around so we were again facing the expansive hue of sky and water.

"Dude, lighten up." He gave my shoulders a little shake.

You'd think Chunk calling me dude would bother me, but he called everyone dude. Even his fellow mathletes, which always struck me as a kind of funny juxtaposition.

He always talked to guys and girls in the same gender-blind way.

"That there is some fine H2O. The sun is shining, narwhals

are out there somewhere, breeding, making little sea unicorns, and we'll be free of Kennedy soon. What more do you want?" he asked, but gave me no time to speak. "Don't answer that. This day is perfection."

I shrugged.

"The word was *perfection*," he said, indicating a game of synonyms. Clearly he'd hoped to distract me.

"Flawless," I said.

"Peerless," he said.

I thought for a second. "Unequaled."

He came back with "Matchless."

"You win," I told him, and presented my upper arm. He punched it, which is what the winner gets to do.

Chunk almost always wins when we play this game. He made it up, and I think he secretly designed it to try to make me smarter or something. Not that I'm complaining, since I credit my excellent verbal SAT score to it.

Chunk himself was one of only a few hundred people in the US to get a perfect score of 2400. He's the smartest guy I know, valedictorian, headed off to Stanford in the fall.

"Of course I won," he said, stepping away from me. He'd never been shy about how smart he was, either. Neither of us is a terribly popular person. "Just one more thing."

The ocean breeze cooled my shoulder where his arm had been.

"About the wedding," he said. "Think road trip."

And he leaned way back so I couldn't slug him.

He broke the code of Black Hole, but I was so surprised by the words *road trip*, I didn't even try.

"As in you and me? Driving to Chicago together?"

"Sure." He grinned. "Imagine the adventure! Ratty motels, junk food, awesome playlists, bizarro roadside attractions!"

"Who are you and what have you done with my friend?" I demanded.

He looked away. "I have an inexplicable hankering to see these great United States."

I saw long days of driving, the open road stretching out in front of us, like some final frontier. We'd play trivia games, and Truth, and Spot the Out-of-State License Plates.

And then there was the opportunity to demonstrate to my dad the effect seven months of hormone therapy had had so far.

A wave crashed over the head of a guy with a silvery blue boogie board, and I flashed on another image of me showing up to my dad's wedding, only this time in a dress the color of that board. I pictured the shock of recognition on Dad's face . . . I'd show *him* a phase.

But then I faltered. Would the other guests know anything about me? What would I say to Jan? Would I pass as a girl? And if not, would it be unsafe to drive across the country?

The boogie boarder popped up behind the wave, and I looked over at Chunk. He was staring intently out at the horizon. I thought about milk shakes in diners and nights in kitschy motels. Hanging out and watching bad TV, just the two of us.

"We'd take Betty the Car?" I asked.

"Unless you have a car of your own you've been keeping a secret all this time." His lips curved in a half smile, and his cheek dimple deepened.

I tried to sound cool. "It would be kind of a last hurrah before I go to New York and you go off to Stanford . . ."

"Right?" Chunk pulled out his phone and checked the calendar. "And we have exactly five and a half weeks to teach you to drive stick."

"Who am I to deny my friend the opportunity to see these great United States?" I asked the ocean.

As if that was the only reason I was agreeing to go.

CHAPTER 2

When I get to Chunk's, he's still in his room. His parents have already left for work, and I wonder if they subjected him to the same wear-your-seat-belt-and-sunscreen-and-be-safe lecture I had from my mom.

He's the youngest of four, so probably not. His older siblings have already broken his parents in when it comes to stuff like this.

His sister, Pandora, home on summer break from Princeton (Chunk's whole family is smart), lets me in.

I look down to make sure the hoodie covers everything.

It's not so much that I'd mind Pandora knowing about my transition, it's that I don't want anyone telling Chunk's mom until after I leave for school.

I'm sure Dr. Kefala's a good psychiatrist, but I'm not one of her patients.

My freshman year when I came out as gay (this was before *trans* was even a word in my vocabulary) she *tortured* me with understanding, compassion, and many, many attempted conversations about what I was feeling and how I was doing. She even started a diversity task force at our school.

Wayyyy too much focus coming from the mom of your best friend, you know?

When Pandora gives me a hug, I make my chest concave and step out of her embrace as quickly as possible, under the pretext of giving her the once-over.

She's wearing a gigantically baggy men's oxford shirt open to reveal a tight camisole printed with the Princeton logo. Skinny capri-length pants show off the bottom part of her toned calves, and scuffed penny loafers complete the ensemble. Her thick black hair is full and tousled; her style is at once preppy and disheveled.

"You look great," I tell her, and she smiles hugely.

When girls see me as a gay guy, my compliments on style and appearance seem to take on a special significance. Kind of an "Oh, Jeremy's gay; he must have great taste" thing.

I know it'll change when they know the compliment is coming from another girl, and one with no discernable style of her own at that.

In any case, preppy-disheveled is a great look on Pandora, but I couldn't pull it off. My ankles are too thin and my shoulders too broad. I'd look like a cross between a scarecrow and prep school reject in that outfit.

She steps back and points to two huge five-gallon buckets that say PEARSON'S CUSTOM STAIN-AND-SEAL on their sides.

"I'm supposed to remind you both to drop those off in Tahoe. That way maybe at least one of you will remember."

Chunk's parents are having some work done on their

cabin, and since Tahoe is on our way to Chicago, they want us to drop by and check on things. Like either of us knows a thing about deck building.

"Don't they have deck stain in Tahoe?"

"Custom color," she says.

"'Keydoke," I say, dropping my duffel bag and laptop case on top of the buckets and heading upstairs to Chunk's immaculate bedroom.

I mean pristine. The books on his bookshelf are arranged alphabetically by author, and I know his dirty clothes are in the hamper instead of being strewn around on the floor, as they should be in a normal teenager's room.

Chunk is sitting at his desk in front of the computer he built himself, and there are a million chat windows open. He belongs to more online forums than I can shake a joystick at.

Most of the people he chats with are people he has never met in person. People with screen names like Twizzler and Ghouliath and Lizard. People with no lives, who just happen to share his interests in gaming, old-time cartoons, liberal politics, and science.

"We're already late," I say, from the doorway.

He's the one who broke down the timing of the trip. According to the interwebs we can get on Interstate 80 and just stay there until we reach Chicago. Under normal traffic conditions it should only take thirty-three hours or so.

Who knew?

His idea is to do it in three eleven-hour days of driving, taking turns at the wheel. I've only ever driven my mom's automatic, so he gave me a few lessons on driving stick, and I think I did pretty well.

Except for a teeny-tiny tendency to stall out at stop signs. I'm sure I'll improve.

Coming back, we'll take things at a more leisurely pace along Interstate 40 because, hey! There's a place called Dinosaur, Colorado, and who could pass up *that*?

"We need to leave now if we're going to make it to Salt Lake City in time for a night of bad TV."

"Just finishing up," he says, not taking his eyes off the screen, but holding a bunch of papers out to me. I come into the room and take them. They're printouts of American roadside attractions. I flip through.

"Ghost towns and animatronic presidents? Padlock your love in Lovelock, Nevada?" I ask. "Can we see all of these just off I-80? I want to leave plenty of time for kitschy motel relaxation."

"Don't get your undies in a twist." He's typing something lightning fast. "We'll pick the best ones, drop in for fifteen minutes, and be on our way. For the most part, they're all really close to the highway." He stops typing and glances over at me (finally) before turning back to his computer.

I flop onto his bed. Have I mentioned that the more you try to hurry him the slower he goes?

"I'm not sure we need to see the shoes made from the skin of Big Nose George," I say, reading from the printout.

Chunk doesn't look away from his screen.

"It'll be fun," he says.

"You're saying it'll be fun to see a pair of shoes made from human skin."

"Maybe not," he says, distracted.

I busy myself reading about the roadside attractions until he turns away from the computer, a video camera in his hand.

Aiming the lens at himself, he says, "Captain's Log, Stardate 11706.14."

What??? "We really need to get going." It's almost ten o'clock. "What is that?"

Chunk clears his throat. "My dad's old camera. Recording our epic adventure."

I whip out my phone and start filming him with it. "And the reason you don't just use your phone?"

"I'm all about the retro." He turns the camera around so he's filming me filming him.

"Besides, this way I thought you could film some and I could film some. It'll all be in one place so when my phone dies and *yours* gets lost, we'll still have this valuable record of our epic adventure. When we're old and gray, we can show it to our grandkids."

"You can show it to yours. No grandkids for me, remember?" Chunk knows I don't want kids.

Chunk turns his camera back on himself. "First mate getting testy."

I smile at the stupid pun, but my mom wouldn't.

Sterility was a huge thing she worried about when I talked to her about transitioning. She told Dr. E she was afraid that if she okayed hormones that'd make me unable to have kids,

I might change my mind when I'm older, want them, and blame her for letting me transition.

"Fertility is more a concern in individuals who've gone from hormone blockers to hormones, bypassing the puberty of their birth sex assignments entirely," Dr. E told her. "In any case, better a sterile adult who's mad at you than a dead kid," he said, and handed her a card printed with information for TNet, a group for parents and families of trans people. "And there's always adoption."

"Our mission: to go where no man has gone before," Chunk intones.

I make a harrumphing noise.

"Sorry. To boldly go where no *human* has gone before."

"How 'bout a little less *Trek*, a little more gender-neutrality, and a lot more get this show on the road?"

"The time has come," he agrees, powering down his desktop. Finally.

- - - - - - -

The containers of stain-and-seal have to go into Betty's back hatch on their sides. Pandora comes out to the driveway and helps us arrange our luggage in a way that will keep them from rolling around. There's my stuff plus Chunk's backpack, his laptop case, and a bag of DVDs in case cable at the kitschy motels disappoints. The last things to go in are our matching Space Camp duffel bags. The hatch just barely closes.

"Sleeping in the car at night has just been ruled out as an option." Pandora smiles.

"It never was," I assure her.

"Gotcha." She gives Chunk a hug. "Stay away from the Bates Motel."

She's referring to a movie she showed me and Chunk the Halloween we were eleven. It's about a creepy hotel where the psycho owner keeps his dead mom's body and dresses up in her clothes and kills a girl in a shower. The girl getting stabbed in the shower freaked Chunk out, but what gave me nightmares was the guy dressing up in his skeleton-mom's clothes.

Go figure.

"Our reservations are at the Bucket of Blood," Chunk tells her. She chuckles.

"Except for the one night we have planned at the Clown-of-Death Honeymoon Inn and Suites," I say, and then feel stupid when she doesn't laugh right away.

"Or someplace even scarier." I try separating the romance from the creep.

She turns to hug me, and I go through the shoulder-hunch-concave-chest routine.

"You guys be careful."

"We will," I promise even as a bolt of nervous energy shoots through me. Not every place we're driving through is exactly LGBTQ friendly. I will be very, very careful.

Pandora heads back into the house, and Chunk and I get into Betty. I arrange the sack of essential food I brought (snack-size bag of Doritos, powdered Donettes, sunflower seeds, and a six-pack of Dr Pepper) by my feet while he attaches a clip to the dash for the camcorder. When he's done with that he reaches behind his seat, pulls out a little plastic bag, and hooks the handles to the glove compartment.

"For trash."

I manage not to roll my eyes. Chunk loves Betty the Car; keeping her clean is super important. We weren't allowed to even eat in her the first six months he had her.

His mom wanted to buy him a Prius, and his dad thought he should get a used Mercedes sedan. Chunk looked at *Consumer Reports* and talked to people online. He said that a Prius just shouted "Look at me, I care about the environment!" and that the Mercedes shouted "Look at me, I care about money!" He decided on the Honda Insight.

The day he got the car, he drove over to my house, crowing. He was excited about his new ride but not in the way most normal people are thrilled about their first vehicles.

Below is an excerpt of the actual conversation we had when I got into his car for the first time:

Chunk: "The Insight is perfect. Not too image-y, gets fifty-six miles to the gallon, and the insurance is cheaper because it's an older model!"

Me: "I will call her Betty the Car."

Chunk spent the last few weeks giving me lessons in driving stick. And I love Betty the Car despite her many flaws, like having to turn off the air-conditioning when going uphill, or the fact that the metal doohickey for holding her hood up is missing, so there's a long, fat stick dedicated to that purpose always rattling around in the back hatch.

Now she's going to cocoon me and Chunk all the way to Chicago, so I love her even more.

– – – – – – –

Before he starts Betty, Chunk plugs in his phone, turns on the camcorder, and says, "Captain's Log, Stardate 11706.14. To infinity and beyond."

"Do you think real Trekkies would be stoked about a *Toy Story* mash-up?" I wonder aloud.

When we pull out of the driveway the skin on the back of my neck prickles in a good way. This street I've walked down thousands of times looks different somehow. I imagine the houses looking at me and even though I'm still wearing my fly-under-the-radar clothes, I imagine I'll look different to them when I come back.

We're off.

I stick my face in front of the camera. I try on my new voice, which is higher, more breathy.

"To infinity and beyond."

CHAPTER 3

It turns out there's a hellish amount of traffic on the way to infinity.

The sun is hot and bright through the driver's-side window, and there's a sweaty sheen on Chunk's upper lip. We've been on the road for almost three hours, which feels crazy considering the short distance we've traveled. It seems like the entire Bay Area must be headed for points East today. And now there's the torturous, air conditioner–less climb up I-680 toward the Benicia Bridge.

"When the road flattens out, we can switch," I offer.

"We'll see," he says.

An old song, "Glitter in the Air," comes up on the playlist, and I sing along.

I was around ten when P!nk performed it at the Grammys, twirling and twisting on a silk trapeze. I begged for gymnastics lessons after that, but my dad would have none of it, and in this rare instance my mom didn't argue with him.

"You already have Scouts and Little League," he had said.

The fact that I hated both didn't bother him a bit. I retaliated by cutting my bedsheets in half so I could at least wrap myself up like P!nk when she had been suspended in the air above the audience members' heads, singing about feeding lovers with just her hand.

Aunt Jan was over when the ruined sheets were discovered. I said I'd done it for art, having learned early on that the one way to get my mom and Jan on my side against my dad was for me to call any mess I made art. It never failed me.

Jan was:

1) Assistant curator of modern and contemporary art at the Silicon Valley Art Museum
2) An art teacher at the Academy of Design
3) The person who stole my dad
4) All of the above

— — — — — — —

P!nk ends and Mumford and Sons comes on. Before P!nk we had forty minutes of Koji Kondo, video game music composer. "You put together one eclectic playlist," I compliment Chunk.

He nods, focused on spurring Betty the Car up the Sunol Grade. The air conditioner is off in the hopes of getting her to go faster. Right now he's flooring it, and we're going about thirty-nine miles an hour.

I do not have high hopes for the Rockies.

I know better than to mention that.

"The word was *eclectic*," I say.

Chunk downshifts. "Diverse."

"Varied."

He frowns at that; it must have been the word he was planning to use. "All-embracing" is what he comes back with.

"I don't think that counts," I tell him. "Two words."

"I disagree. Just put a *p* by my name for *protest*," he says, and then throws out "Multifarious."

Even when he's focused on something else, like getting to the top of a hill without Betty the Car quitting on us, he wins.

I dig into the junk food bag as an eighteen-wheeler pulls around us. It's the open kind, heaped in the back with tons and tons of shiny, ripe tomatoes. My stomach grumbles a little.

"Jesus, it's bad when even the trucks are passing our fat ass," I say. "Here, have a Donette," and I pull out the last one and try to give it to Chunk, who doesn't take his hands off the wheel.

Eyes glued to the road, he says, "No, thanks."

"Sure you don't want it?"

"I said no!"

I was warned that the hormones would make me "sensitive" and that what my body is telling my brain is that it's PUBERTY TIME!!! Which means I'm like a thirteen-year-old girl when it comes to highs and lows.

"Fine." I stare out the passenger window, trying not to cry.

We listen to music in silence, and a little later Chunk grabs a bag of sunflower seeds from the center console and struggles to open it with one hand, using his teeth.

I don't offer to help him.

Fifteen minutes later we finally pull up to the toll plaza. I unbuckle my seat belt, reach into the Space Camp bag for my wallet, and grab the hundred-dollar bill Luanne, my boss at Fabrics Galore, gave me for graduation. I worked there for almost two years, until just a week ago in fact, and I really liked it. Once in a while a customer could be kind of a pain, but I felt like Luanne always had my back.

Chunk takes the money to hand over to the toll taker. She's wearing blue surgical gloves like the ones I once shoved into Betty's glove compartment because hey, a glove compartment should have gloves.

"Yagotanythingsmallerthanthis?" she asks.

"I'm sorry, what?" Chunk asks.

"Ya gotanythingsmaller than *this*?" She gives the hundred-dollar bill a shake.

Chunk looks pointedly over his stomach and down at his crotch like he's checking out the size of his . . . anatomy.

"Nope," he says.

I can't help it. Even though I'm still pissed at Chunk, I laugh.

She rolls her eyes and counts the change back into Chunk's hand. He stuffs ninety-four bucks into the ashtray, shifts, and then turns on the camcorder.

"Captain's Log, Stardate 11706.14. Low-level minions of the Benicia sector lack developed senses of humor," he says.

And just like that, all is good again.

After the Benicia Bridge Chunk pulls off the road so I can drive. We climb out of Betty and stand for a minute looking out at a group of old ships, anchored side by side in Suisun Bay. They're called the mothball fleet.

I've passed by these ships from the time I was a kid but I don't know anything about them other than their name.

"How long have they been here?" I ask, secure in the knowledge that he'll be able to tell me.

Chunk spits out a sunflower seed shell. "Since just after World War II. The Navy decommissioned and packed 'em away here."

"They look so sad."

Chunk cracks another seed between his teeth and says around it, "I read that people who anthropomorphize things suffer from a lack of deep social connection with others."

I ignore him. We've had this conversation before. Both his parents are psychiatrists, and I swear, trying to analyze everyone and everything is a Kefala family trait, passed down in the DNA.

I'm about to point out that his social connections are mostly on the Internet and don't count, when he says, "In a couple years all of those ships'll be gone. Torn apart for scrap."

"That's supposed to make me feel better?"

He punches me lightly on the shoulder. "Cheer up! They'll be recycled so they'll still exist. Matter doesn't just disappear. They'll be around in one way or another forever."

He hands me the keys and I get to drive.

Finally.

The road isn't as steep, and traffic is much better than it was on 680. We should make it to the cabin in Tahoe in under three hours. We're just going to drop off the stain-and-seal, check on things, and take off again. I want to hit Salt Lake City tonight and leave early in the morning before it gets too light. In a place like Utah, I feel like the dark is a friend to someone who might be at an ambiguous-looking point gender-wise.

When it comes to passing, of all the things I curse about my body, I curse the follicles on my face the most. I'll have to be stupid careful about shaving.

I learned to use an old-fashioned straight-edge razor because I read it gives a much closer shave than a disposable one. I just recently managed to get over the accidentally-slicing-up-my-skin-and-walking-around-with-toilet-paper-stuck-to-my-chin phase.

I swear my individual facial hairs are like tiny toothpicks that have a secret plan to unite and form a billboard that says THIS GIRL WAS BORN WITH A PENIS!!! BEAT THE CRAP OUT OF HER!

"How about a game of trivia?" I ask, to keep from thinking about it anymore.

CHAPTER 4

Three hours later the sun's faded to that delicious late-afternoon shade it brews up during the summer. Just after Sacramento, we gorged ourselves from the drive-thru at In-N-Out Burger and I'm:

1) Driving

2) Almost in a food coma

3) Very glad we're not too far away from the cabin

We just finished up a game of Truth, which is basically just asking each other questions from an app on Chunk's phone called Tell Me About It. There is no dare. Categories are things like Romance, Friendship, Family, and Death and Taxes. I guess it's not really even a game, although if you think the other person is lying, you get to slug them in the arm.

Did I mention that most of the games we play have some sort of punching in them?

We pass a sign that says SAFE AND SANE FIREWORKS.

"No one ever advertises the other kind," Chunk complains. "I like the Dangerous and Insane fireworks myself."

I downshift, thinking back to the first piece in my portfolio.

White
7x10 inches
> Image: Red lips devour white fireworks on deep blue background, portrait of the artist adrift in the margin.
> Acrylic on paper

Late-afternoon sun slanted through the trees and lit up the grass, making patches of warm green laced with shadier kelly green. The smell of the brownies for the neighborhood block party floated out through the back windows of our house. All day long my mom'd worn her good-mom face. The one that made me want to snuggle up with her, kiss her, be like her.

My dad was in a good mood too. He'd come home from somewhere or other with a bag of fireworks, and he and I were hanging out in the backyard. All was perfect in my four-year-old world.

Dad put a sparkler in my hand and kneeled behind me, helping me hold it away from myself before he actually lit it. The sudden crackly buzz and sulfury smell scared and excited me at the same time. Sparks, white with heat, danced off of the slender stick in my hand.

Frightening, beautiful.

I stared, mesmerized, for I don't know how long, but

the thing had burned down pretty far by the time my mom came barreling out of the house and I looked up.

The dress she wore must have been retro even then, tight sleeveless bodice, blue, full, knee-length swishy skirt. You know, the kind of dress you see in '50s vintage-looking memes that say supposedly outrageous things like "Is it vodka o'clock yet?"

"What the hell are you doing? Don't give him that!" Even yelling, my mom's mouth was beautiful. Bright red lipstick made her teeth even whiter.

My dad held me closer with one arm. "We're fine out here."

"Put it out! Damn it! Who gives a four-year-old fireworks?" she screamed.

"What? I'm right here! Quit overreacting!"

The sparkler burned out and my dad stood up, letting go of my hand.

"Jesus! Edward! You're the worst goddamn father ever!"

"Shut up! Jeremy handled it just fine; he's a big boy." My dad patted my head and I dropped the still-smoldering sparkler onto my bare foot.

Now it was my turn to scream, and my mom rushed down from the porch to take a look. The mark from the burn was small, but I remember the shock of it and the pain. She scooped me up, rushed me into the house, and stuck my foot under the kitchen faucet.

"You're okay, you're okay," she crooned over and over, scooping cold water over my foot with her hand.

After several minutes the pain went from excruciating to just bad.

"Is that better, honey?" I nodded and she turned off the faucet. I still sat on the kitchen counter, foot in the sink. My father stood in the doorway, useless and shamed.

"I want another sparkler," I said, even though I didn't.

I just wanted the day to go back to being good.

The look on my mother's face told me my mistake immediately. She stepped away from me and turned on my dad.

"See what you've done, you asshole?" she snarled. "Now he wants to do it again." She pointed to my foot. "Enjoy the boys' club, Jeremy!" she said before slamming out of the kitchen.

What I remember next is sitting by my dad on the couch, foot throbbing in a bowl of cold water, and watching my mom through the picture window that looked out on our backyard.

She leaned against the porch railing in her heavenly blue dress, smoking cigarette after skinny cigarette in short angry puffs. There was the sound of a baseball game on TV, and of hot white fireworks in the distance.

The words *boys' club* cycled through my head, and I felt banished.

CHAPTER 5

Chunk closes the Tell Me app and puts down his phone. It's almost five o'clock, we've exited I-80 onto Highway 89, and the cabin's not too far away.

"So, do you have a plan for the wedding yet?" he asks.

I pretend to think about it for a minute. "Yeah, it involves turning around at the Iowa-Illinois border."

I mostly keep my gaze on the road but kind of look at him out of the corner of my eye to see his reaction. What would he do if I chickened out?

"No, really," he says, not even considering the option. "I think you should come up with a game plan."

"I have one . . . it involves a lot of duct tape, a llama, and a peanut butter sandwich."

Chunk grins. "You don't even know what you mean by that, do you?"

"Not a clue," I agree, smiling. I love making him laugh, even when it means saying stupid things.

"Maybe it'd help if you figured out your objective here," he says.

"*My* objective? You're the one who thinks this is necessary for my development as a human being. I'm pretty much along for the roadside attractions and junk food."

Which is the truth, but not all of it.

There is the whole making-my-dad-see-me-as-female—as the person I really am—thing.

But I don't want to think about that right now. I want to experience weird sights and kitschy motels and being with Chunk.

He's stubborn, though.

"Fine, let's talk about what your objective is *not* and come at it from that angle."

"Okay, logic boy." I give in.

"It's not to break up the wedding, right?" he asks. "I mean it's not like you want your parents to get back together."

"God, no!" My parents were truly horrible together. I am not exaggerating when I say that I cannot recall a single family outing that did not end up in a fight of some sort or another.

She was being bitchy.

He was being passive-aggressive.

Could he please stop ogling the waitress?

Could she please stop being crazy?

"You know if I had a time machine, I'd use it to go back and make sure they never met."

"Then you wouldn't exist," Chunk says, a little smug, like he thinks he got me.

I shrug. "Maybe, maybe not. It could be that I'd still exist, just in a different way, kind of like you said the mothball fleet will still exist, just not in the same form."

Like, I'd still have my mentality, but I'd be in a different body. One that would match up with the way I experience gender.

"Wait, are you talking about physically?" he asks.

"I guess I'm mostly talking about consciousness," I say.

"So we're talking about the soul."

I keep my eyes on the road.

The word *soul* makes me feel shy about nodding yes. I've always stayed away from conversations about spirituality with Chunk. I don't want him to rag on me because it can't be scientifically proven, but even if I don't go as far as my crazy mom—and he and I both laugh behind her back when she comes out saying things like "Go with Spirit and you can't go wrong"—I like to think that an existence outside of the bodies we're in is possible.

I don't want him to try talking me out of it either, even if I'm not a hundred percent sure of what I believe myself. If I need to defend my conclusions once I've reached them, I'm fine, but I just want the chance to come to them on my own.

Having a genius best friend is a bitch that way.

"I guess," I mutter.

We're headed up another hill and he reaches over to turn off the air conditioner before rolling down his window. Leaning back, he says the perfect thing. "Anything's possible."

— — — — — —

We follow 89 until we come to West Lake Boulevard. We pass trees and a campground and trees and a shopping center and more trees. To our right there are snatches of blue lake, seen in between the trees. It's a lot of trees.

And it's beautiful.

"Turn up ahead," he says, and I do without stalling. His family's place sits across the street from the beachfront houses in a subdivision of vacation homes.

We pull up under the wooden deck that covers part of the driveway, Chunk grabs the trash bag so he can empty it, and we get out.

When he unlocks the door and we step inside, the cool of the house contrasted with the heat of the car makes me shiver. There are old-fashioned skis hanging over the entryway, but the furniture in the living room betrays the cabin as more of a summery hangout. Kitschy '50s-style signs with bathing beauties diving off docks that say things like "Welcome to the Lake" and "Tahoe! Adventures begin here!" hang on the finished wood walls.

The slipcovers on the couch and chairs match the drapes, with their giant cabbage roses and bluebells. Truthfully, it looks like a bridal bouquet threw up in here. I catch myself wondering what Jan has chosen for her own bouquet. It's too late in the season for lilacs, her favorite flower.

Not that I care.

"Let me just check on a few things, unload the stain-and-seal, and call my mom. Then we can get out," Chunk says, heading straight through the living room and kitchen and out the back door, where he grabs a metal doohickey and uses it to twist an X-shaped piece sticking out of the ground next to the steps.

He comes back inside and turns on the tap over the kitchen sink.

A deep rumbling issues forth before the water comes pouring out.

"Is there anything I can do?" I ask, not out of a genuine desire to help as much as a genuine desire to get back on the road quickly.

"Go sit on the deck while I turn on the rest of the faucets." Chunk's family keeps the water turned off during the winter so the pipes don't freeze, and between all of the bajillion senior honors banquets he and his parents had to attend in the spring and graduation, I guess no one's been to the cabin since last fall.

I walk out to the deck, which is bigger than I remember it being. Or maybe I'm just looking at it from the staining and sealing perspective, a job I'd hate to have.

Pulling the cover off a wrought-iron chair, I sit down and put my feet up on the railing. Early-evening sun is warm on my skin, and in front of me the blue jewel that is Lake Tahoe spreads out. There are some boats in the distance, and a lone paddleboarder in the foreground. I take my phone out and snap a picture in case I want to use the scene in a watercolor sometime.

Chunk comes out the sliding glass door, the cabin's phone pressed to his ear.

"Naw, it all looks good, Ma. Uh-huh." He listens for a

minute, makes the international signal for yacking with his right hand. "Uh-huh. The flowering quince?"

He peers over the edge of the deck.

"Um—there's, like, brown sticks down there or something . . . They will? Oh, okay. J," he says, calling me by the name we agreed he'd use around his mom and bringing me back from a place I'd gone to tune out their domestic chat. "Go down there and turn on the hose and water those plants, okay?"

I cock my head at him like, *really?* He inclines his head and makes the yacking motion with his hand again. "Uh-huh, I'll check on it," he's saying into the phone.

I go down the outside stairs of the deck to a planter box that has brown sticks that are meant to be flowers, I guess. I turn on the spigot next to the box. It takes a minute for a rusty-colored water to run out of the hose.

"Yoo-hoo!" I look up to see a little old lady shuffling toward me from one of the houses across the street. According to Chunk's parents, those houses cost a fortune—to buy or to rent, and there's something a little incongruous about the way this little old lady wears a shabby housecoat with giant begonias on it and slippers of the kind you'd expect to see on the feet of people in a senior care facility.

I feel a little caught out myself. The car was hot, so I'm just wearing a T-shirt and jeans. No sports bra to squish things down, no sweatshirt to hide my shape. I run a hand over my jaw and don't feel stubble. Still, I hunch my shoulders.

"Yoo-hoo!" she calls out again. She has a cane, and it

seems mean to make her come all the way up the driveway.

"Hey!" I call up to Chunk. "There's someone here!"

He pops his head over the edge of the deck, phone still to his ear, and looks toward the old lady.

"Okay, okay, Ma, I'll check. Look, I gotta go, Mrs. Harris is here. Mmhmm—I'll tell her you said hi. Uh-huh. Love you, too." I hear the beep when he hangs up. He thunders down the outside stairs.

"Hi, Mrs. Harris!" He could not sound more delighted. "How are you?" He crosses the driveway and kisses her on the cheek like he's this debonair Frank Sinatra type. This makes me melt a little.

Mrs. Harris turns to look at me.

"And who is this?" she asks. I breathe deep, cross the asphalt, and shake her hand. It's tiny, the size and shape of a bony bird's wing. My hand feels enormous, like a paw around hers. Does she notice?

"This is Jess," Chunk says. "I don't think you've met before."

"I'm the neighborhood watch around here," Mrs. Harris cackles. "Watching the comings and goings!" She turns to Chunk, kind of brandishing her cane. "I came running over to let you know there's been a bear around here, so you need to be real careful with the trash."

"Will do," Chunk says. And they stand there talking for a few minutes about bear boxes and people I don't know—who's here for the summer, who's renting their house out instead. The conversation moves on to how Mrs. Harris needs help with something. I'm discreetly checking the time on my phone when I hear Chunk say, "Sure, we'll give you a hand!"

It's after five, and there's still Scheels Sportsman Attraction to check off the roadside attraction list today.

The word *sport* in the title "Scheels Sportsman Attraction" does nothing for either of us, but according to Chunk's printout, Scheels is a gigantic mall outside of Reno that's managed to cram all kinds of crazy into 295,000 square feet of space.

The plan is to skip the indoor rifle range (duh) but there's an indoor mountain with stuffed elk and bears we want to check out, in addition to something called the Walk of Presidents, featuring fourteen animatronic presidents positioned around the railing of the second floor. There's also a sixty-five-foot Ferris wheel *inside* the mall.

Chunk really wants to see which presidents the mall owners decided to immortalize, and I want us to buy fudge at the "world famous" candy store, and ride on the Ferris wheel. (It seems doubtful that the ride maintenance at Scheels is taken care of by toothless crack addicts.)

If we're going to experience the magic and wonder of this mall and still make it to Salt Lake City in time to enjoy bad TV and kitschy motel time, we need to get on the road.

Still, I'm nodding and saying to Mrs. Harris, "Of course we can help."

"Are you sure you don't mind?"

"Not at all," Chunk says with a smile. And then we're shuffling across the street with Mrs. Harris at a glacial pace.

We get to her house and it's enormous. "Too big for one

person," she says. "But the children come visit me and bring the grandkids, so it's nice to have space for the young hellions."

Chunk dutifully asks about her kids and grandkids, and I dutifully refrain from checking the time on my phone yet again.

She opens the door on a huge foyer, and stacked inside it are millions and millions of boxes.

"My girl, Linda, comes day after tomorrow and I could have her move them, but I'm beginning to feel like a hoarder. I just need them to go into the library. They're books."

To my credit and to Chunk's, neither of us groans.

The thing is, since I started taking hormones, I've lost some upper body strength. Still, my dainty upper arms do manage to help him move all million (okay, twenty-four) boxes of books from the foyer into the library.

Scheels and Salt Lake City are calling my name the whole time.

When the last box has been stacked, Mrs. Harris follows us to the front of the house.

"I'm afraid I've already eaten. Old people's hours, you know," she says. "Or I'd give you dinner."

"No, no, that's very generous, but we need to get going," Chunk tells her.

We've just opened the door to leave when she says to Chunk in a loud whisper, "Now, your parents *do* know she's here, don't they?"

Chunk assures her that they do.

"Well, off you go, then," she says. "You two have a wonderful date."

I glance at Chunk to see how he takes this. He blinks, but I can't read his face. I step over the threshold, and when we're just out of Mrs. Harris's line of sight, I give him an exaggerated wink. He doesn't respond except to tell her to have a nice night.

We get back on the road and I can't stop smiling.

Sure she was old and infirm and probably had bad eyesight from reading too many books, but I passed!

The fact she thought Chunk and I were together makes me smile even harder. Good old Chunk.

Red
14x17 inches
> Image: Portrait of the artist as anime figure Sailor
> Moon, bursting through a sheet of paper, crushing
> faceless male figure in her hand.
> Acrylic, torn vellum, yellowed Scotch tape on canvas

I've known Chunk since kindergarten. But we didn't really hang out until we were in third grade.

The huge excitement at the beginning of that year was that we were going to finally get to use the computer lab at school. I can't even remember what the lesson was about, and it didn't make much difference. We all had computers at home but there was something cool about getting to use the ones at school, and even cooler about getting to use the color printers in the lab.

A bunch of us were into anime and manga and spent the free time after we finished our work looking up and printing out pictures. I made the mistake of printing out my favorite, Sailor Moon.

The picture had an interesting perspective from above. You could see she was gesturing with her left hand, her right was on her hip, and her ropy long blond pigtails flared out from the sides of her head and then extended down to the tops of her shiny, knee-high red boots.

This kid named Cole Billings caught sight of the picture and when the bell rang for us to return to our regular classroom, he grabbed it out of my hands. Easy to do—I was super small for my age.

"Look, everyone, Jeremy's favorite is Sailor Moon!" A couple of the other boys laughed, and I tasted something bitter at the back of my throat. I *did* like Sailor Moon.

I didn't know I wasn't supposed to.

I had no words, nothing to come back with, because by then I *knew* I was different, even if I didn't exactly know how or what it meant. All I knew was that I was always accidently doing the wrong thing around people like Cole Billings. Guys who were the first to the top of the wall when we went rock climbing with the Cub Scouts. The ones who actually liked playing dodgeball and spit great globs of milky saliva onto the ground after they creamed you with the ball.

I knew without needing to look in a mirror that the tips of my ears were redder than Sailor Moon's boots.

Then Chunk stepped in. This was Chunk when he was still Chuck, before the counselor at Space Camp nicknamed him Super-Chunk the summer after seventh grade. (The Super part was a compliment for leading our team to victory in the Tuesday Night Galaxy Trivia Bowl. I don't know about the Chunk part. He was big, but not like he is now—well, obviously not. He's six foot two now, and probably close to two hundred pounds heavier than he was back then. In any case, the nickname stuck, and Chunk didn't seem to mind.)

"So what?" he demanded, folding his arms and squinting at Cole as though Cole was so small he could barely be seen.

"It's a girl thing," Cole said.

"It doesn't have to be," Chunk argued. "My mom and dad are psychiatrists—*brain doctors*," he said in an exaggerated way, letting Cole and his friends know he thought they were too stupid to understand what psychiatrists were. "And they say people can like whatever they want and whoever they want. It doesn't matter if you're a boy or a girl."

Cole, still holding my printout, ripped it in half, threw it on the ground, and turned around to leave the computer lab.

"C'mon, we'll fix this," Chunk said, picking up the pieces of my Sailor Moon printout like he maybe didn't recognize that I had just been exposed, or maybe he didn't care.

I followed him back to our regular class, where he gravely informed Mr. Porter that we needed some tape because, and I'll never forget him using these exact words, "some unfortunate business has occurred."

The other words that stuck with me through the years are the obvious ones.

People can like whatever they want and whoever they want.

Chunk and I were both in Cub Scouts along with Danny Zim, Joey Blanca, Bill Yang, and the hated Cole Billings. We had a Scout meeting that afternoon, and when it was over, Chunk and I walked to his house to play Dungeons & Dragons and paint Warhammers.

From then on it was always me and Chunk.

— — — — — —

When we cross the border from California to Nevada, there's just enough daylight to see that we have left all green behind. The landscape becomes brown and barren. Seriously, it's like when they went to draw state lines, the people in charge of Nevada lost all the trees in a poker game or something.

iTunes is on shuffle and I'm driving and sort of singing along to some of the songs.

Chunk's been quiet since we left the cabin.

Isn't there some road trip rule that when one person's driving, it's the job of the passenger to keep them entertained so they don't fall asleep and crash?

"Nevada could use some glamming," I tell him, when we leave the Sierras behind.

"That's what Vegas is for," he says, yawning.

"Kind of funny that Mrs. Harris thought we were together," I say, watching him from the corner of my eye.

"Meh," he says.

"We should have told her we had a date in Salt Lake City." I laugh to show I'm joking.

"What, tonight?"

I swallow, and give Betty the Car too much gas without shifting. She whines until I lift my foot.

"There's no way we're doing anything in Salt Lake tonight." His voice has an edge. "It's after eight now. We're getting in at, like, four in the morning. Shift."

I obey and Betty the Car settles down.

Chunk pulls out his phone and starts typing. I think he's looking something up, but then I hear the *swoosh* of a text coming in.

The thought of a cozy evening, holed up in some retro motel watching bad TV, slips away. And he didn't, even in a joking way, address the whole Mrs.-Harris-thinks-we're-together thing.

Tap tap tap go his fingers.

"I don't think it's a good idea to drive until then," I tell him. "That's eight straight hours of driving."

"You're the one who wanted to slip in and out of Salt Lake under the cover of night," he reminds me, not looking up.

"That was before I realized the dangers of highway hypnosis," I say like I'm doing a driver's ed video voice-over. *Swoosh* goes his phone.

"Besides, what about Scheels? I think we should go there, then stop for the night and make it up tomorrow."

Tap tap tap. Swoosh.

"Scheels will be closed by the time we get there," Chunk says.

"What time's it close again?" I ask, thinking of animatronic presidents and stuffed elk and riding a Ferris wheel inside of a mall. But mainly (and I know it's dorky) something about having just passed in front of Mrs. Harris makes me want to try it again. I picture me and Chunk eating fudge in a seat at the top of the Ferris wheel, and people assuming we're a couple.

"The website said nine."

"Sometimes websites lie."

Chunk shakes his head and goes back to typing. He keeps at it, and every so often I hear the incoming text swoosh.

But I don't ask who he's texting.

For the next half hour he's involved enough with his phone that he doesn't notice the billboards advertising Scheels up ahead. In fact, he doesn't look up until I slow down for the turnoff.

"It's 9:20. They're going to be closed," he says, and then it's back to the phone.

"I just want to see," I tell him.

There aren't very many cars in the parking lot, but I refuse to give up hope. After all, the building is huge and the lot is gigantic. Maybe it just looks like not a lot of cars because they're all spread out.

I drive around the complex until I find what must be the main entrance.

When I park, Chunk looks up.

"Really? It's closed, Jess."

"Maybe the stores are closed but they might keep the Ferris wheel open late." I open the door and get out. Chunk turns on the camcorder.

"Captain's Log, Stardate 11706.14. Captain reluctantly following first mate on a pointless mission to prove that planet Scheels is as deserted as it looks."

The entrance is an open-air corridor, on either side of which are storefronts that are indeed closed. We walk along pebbled concrete and Chunk's lagging behind just enough to make it not an adventure we're having together.

We come to a big courtyard. To the left, huge glass doors lead into the mall. In the center of the courtyard there's a larger-than-life bronze statue of a snowboarder performing a death-defying flip.

The whole thing's inverted, with the board and feet—the bulk of the sculpture—up in the air, appearing to defy gravity. The piece is . . . sublime. I step closer, irritation at Chunk's nonengagement falling away. The thought that Jan would appreciate both the art and the subject pops into my head.

Green
8x15 inches
    Image: Redwood tree, shredded bark forms portrait
    of the artist. A female figure stands, back to the
    viewer, away from the tree.
    Mixed media, acrylic, redwood bark on canvas

We sat on our butts in the snow, laughing. My mom and dad were in the lodge drinking grown-up hot cocoa and Jan and I were having a great time without them. I was eleven, and couldn't remember a time that Jan hadn't gone with us on ski vacations. My parents were skiers, but Jan and I were boarders.

We were off to the side near the bottom of a run called Pinball, and we'd both gotten a little air from a mogul and then wiped out in exactly the same way. In the deep wintry powder it hadn't hurt, which is why we were laughing.

Jan's goggles blurred up and she took them off and wiped the inside with her gloved finger, trying to get rid of the condensation. Without her goggles on, you could see her green snowboard jacket matched her eyes perfectly.

"How come Roger didn't come skiing?" I asked, glad he hadn't.

She got a funny look on her face and paused, like she was considering what to tell me.

She swiped her finger along the inside of the goggles again, then said, "He's moving his things out this weekend. We broke up."

She was so matter-of-fact that at first I couldn't tell if she was happy or sad.

Then she looked off down the mountain for a long minute, and I regretted interrupting the fun with a stupid question about Roger's whereabouts. I didn't care where he was.

But she did.

I could tell by the way her shoulders sloped. That morning she'd complained, laughing, that the bulk of her boarding jacket made her look even bigger than she was, but just now, in spite of her almost two hundred pounds, she seemed . . . small. Even her curly hair, escaping from under her beanie, looked bedraggled and sad to me. Across the canyon there were Douglas fir and pine trees. We sat and stared for the longest time.

"Guess what my favorite thing about the redwoods is," I finally said.

She tilted her head, thought for a minute.

"That you're getting really good at drawing them?"

"I like that the bark's the same color as your hair, and the green needles are the color of your eyes."

She got teary.

"Do you know how special you are, Jeremy?" she asked.

Later that night I sat playing my handheld while the adults finished their dinner. When my dad got up to pay the bill, my mom and Jan talked about Roger. Jan had had a couple of glasses of wine, but instead of it making her sad and depressed, she just seemed philosophical.

"Honestly, I don't want to be with someone who doesn't want to be with me," she said, taking a last sip of her wine. "And in the end, really, if a relationship's not right, it's just not meant to be."

— — — — — —

I turn my back on the snowboarder sculpture and face the big glass entrance doors. Chunk pulls at the handle of one, but of course they're locked.

By the time I walk over to peer inside, he's already stepping away. Still I stand there a minute, looking through the glass.

Visions of fudge and Ferris wheels die hard.

When we get back to Betty the Car, Chunk takes the driver's seat without saying anything. I settle into the passenger side and stare out the window.

He heads Betty back onto the highway, and the barren openness of the desert in the dark makes me uncomfortable.

"Should we maybe look up a good place to stop in a few hours?" I ask.

"Sure thing—it's your road trip."

Next to me I feel, rather than see, a familiar shrug. What is his problem? My chest squeezes, and I want to say it's *our* road trip, but I don't.

Instead I go all dork on his ass.

"That's right!" I turn on the camcorder. "Stardate 11706.14. First mate getting ready to research docking facilities. Preferably facilities that have cable. No pool necessary."

I take out my phone and after I've ascertained that Elko, Nevada, is the perfect distance—four hours away, which makes us get in late, but not so late we'll crash in bed right after checking in—I open the Tell Me app for a game of Truth.

Chunk's phone swooshes, and I'm glad he's such a rule-following guy.

He never, ever, ever texts while driving.

"'Category: Family,'" I read. "'Are you more like your mom or your dad?'

"You answer first," I say.

58

"My dad, definitely."

"Really?"

"You don't think so?" he asks, flipping the little doohickey on the rearview mirror that makes it so the headlights coming from behind don't blind the driver.

"I don't know, your dad just seems more into sports and image and fitness and all that," I say.

Chunk's dad plays a lot of tennis and wears a thick gold bracelet. He's a sports fan who never misses a Giants game. And even though he's a psychiatrist, he seems to know when to give it a rest, unlike Chunk's mom.

(Oh, the nightmare of walking into their house a week after I'd admitted being gay to Chunk, saying hi to his mom and getting the first of many Very Meaningful "How are you *feeling*, Jeremy?"s.)

"I see." His face is set, the corners of his mouth turned ever so slightly down. The lopsided dimple that appears when he smiles is nowhere to be seen.

"What?" I ask. There's no mistaking the seeping chill in the car.

"Nothing," he says.

I focus on the road ahead.

"I'm definitely more like my mom," I say.

"No kidding," he says, checking the rearview mirror and speeding up. "I thought the question was more about personality traits. Not physical ones."

"I did, too."

"It sounded like you were just looking at it physically."

"Why would you think that?"

He takes his eyes off the road and gives me a hard look. "I know my mom and I are both . . . big."

This is true, but I'm willing to bet I'm waaaayyy more uncomfortable with my body than he is with his. Besides, I like how he's so solid looking. If you didn't know what a nice guy he is, you might find his size intimidating, like he could beat someone up.

"That's not what I was saying," I protest, and then the implication of what he said a minute ago hits me.

"Wait, you think I resemble my mom *physically*?" I smile because, again, it's not a bad thing.

Chunk lets out an exasperated huff and jabs the radio button on. Static-y Mexican music fills the air, and he turns up the volume.

I turn it down again and pull up another question.

"'Category: Hypothetical.'"

When I see the question, I can't believe my luck.

"'A friend of the same sex, one with whom you've played sports and have had the occasion to share a locker room, comes out to you as gay. Would that change the relationship? Why or why not?'"

"Really?" Chunk asks.

"Really," I say.

"That's a stupid question," he says. "Next."

"You're not going to answer it?"

He shakes his head. "I don't think I need to."

Funny how I'm expected to talk about my feelings, but he isn't.

"You didn't call Black Hole," I say, and punch his arm. Hard.

Maybe he thinks I know the answer, but I want to hear it again.

Tawny
14x17 inches
> **Image: Portrait of the artist gazing through louvered window at the torso of Michelangelo's *David*.**
> **Ink, watercolor on paper**

I sat on the slatted wooden bench in the garden of the old library, *GQ* magazine in my lap. The building had been around since the late 1800s, a smallish stone building, and what it lacked in shelf space, it more than made up for in the grounds that surrounded it. Great louvered windows opened onto a back garden that looked like something out of a French impressionist painting.

We spent a lot of time there during the summer before eighth grade. My house was a battle zone of parental fights interspersed with the sad calm of Mom's chemo weeks, and Chunk's house had bossy older siblings ruling it. Neither of us were the skateboard-in-the-square types, so the library had become our default hangout. Chunk would troll the reference room, looking up obscure bits of information, and I'd sit out in the garden sketching.

Just inside the front door of the building there was a bin where people would bring magazines they'd read and wanted to donate. A lot of times I'd go through the bin looking for collage materials or just to get ideas for stuff to draw or paint.

That summer, someone was always bringing in old issues of *GQ*. Which I loved. I wasn't at all into male fashion, but if anyone asked, I planned to pretend I was.

A tawny-skinned Mediterranean-looking model pouted from the cover of the issue I had in my lap, his tight white jeans so low you could see his hipbones. His lips were full and delicious looking and I was tracing them with my finger when the back the door opened and Chunk stepped out of the library.

He blinked in the sudden bright sunlight, then walked over to sit next to me. I fumbled to shove the *GQ* under my sketchbook, but Chunk stopped me. He took the magazine and flipped through it for a minute.

"You like these guys, huh," he said. Not accusing or teasing, just stating facts.

"They make good models," I said, heart pounding.

"You know they have the IQs of dust mites," he said. "Minuscule."

I licked my lips.

"The word was *minuscule*," he said.

"Small." My heart rate slowed.

"Infinitesimal."

"Tiny."

"Microscopic."

"Really, really small?"

He smiled at that. "But you like 'em anyway."

When I was in fifth grade, I had a dream about kissing Les Michaels, lead singer of the boy band Picante, and I tried to go back to sleep so we could kiss some more. By the time I was in seventh grade I realized I preferred boys to girls, but I never said anything to Chunk. I worried it might make things strange between us, and romantic feelings just weren't something we'd ever talked about.

Until now.

My best friend and I stared at each other for an excruciating minute, and then both turned our heads away.

Stellar's jays made a crazy racket in the tree above us.

"I like looking at them," I finally said.

"It's all good," he said. I glanced over at him and he gave me a little smile. "The only thing I question is your taste, dude."

That night, I slept over at his house. We played Skyrim and ate pizza, and it was all the same as it had been since third grade.

— — — — — —

A *whoosh* signals yet another incoming text on Chunk's phone, and I stare out the windshield. The road between Tahoe and infinity stretches out into the night.

CHAPTER 6

It's almost midnight, and the parking lot of the gas station in Winnemucca, Nevada, is empty. A huge sign illuminates the dark night with that sickly kind of yellow lightbulb people use for bug lights on their porches in the summer.

The road's been flat and Chunk's been driving pretty fast for Chunk, but not as fast as I would. I may not be the best at keeping Betty the Car from stalling out when we're going slow, but I'm definitely a faster driver than he is. Not unsafe, just faster. We're still about an hour and forty minutes away from Elko and he needs to use the bathroom.

I could use some beef jerky.

I pull on my sweatshirt and start to get out of the car. My hood is up, half concealing my face. Chunk shakes his head.

"You look like you're going to rip the place off. You're fine with it down."

I touch my cheek, feeling for stubble, and he must interpret my unease from the gesture because he says, "Or you can wait here, if you want. I'll grab you a Slim Jim."

I nod.

The thing is, I kind of need to pee myself. That should be simple, but instead it leads to a torturous round of do I or don't I?

Wherever possible, I avoid using public restrooms. It feels wrong to use the men's because I'm really not a guy, but at this stage of my transition I worry about using the women's and getting called out for looking too masculine.

So should I be true to myself, or play it safe?

Better just to hold it till we've checked into the motel.

Chunk pushes through the glass doors of the gas station shop. I see him greet the clerk, who hands him a key on what looks like a huge soup ladle.

From the time I have known him, Chunk has always taken longer in the bathroom than anyone I have ever met. Once he took so long that we missed the beginning of a movie we'd gone to see.

Not the coming attractions.

The movie.

I asked him why the hell it always took him forever. What was he doing in there?

He wasn't embarrassed at all. "I just sit and enjoy the human experience," he told me.

I climb into the driver's seat so I can get us to Elko faster than Chunk is willing to drive, then tilt the rearview mirror toward me until I can see my face. My lips are a little chapped and I reach back into my bag for my Burt's Bees tinted lip balm. It's just enough to give a little color without looking obvious like lipstick.

Then I grab my phone to text my mom.

Jess: Hi! Just checking in.

She answers so fast I think she must have had her phone in her hand.

Momster: Oh good! I was just about to put out an APB on you!

Jess: Um . . . U could have called me?

Momster: Oh!!! I hadn't thought of that! ☺ So are you at the hotel in Salt Lake yet?

Jess: Got a late start. Elko tonite. We r all checked in and safe.

(I don't want her to stay up worrying about me.)

Momster: Everything okay?

Jess: Yes. Good night.

Momster: Wait! Are you having fun?

Jess: Yes.

Momster: ☺ Good. Is Chuck having fun too?

Jess: Why wouldn't he be?

Momster: No reason, just asking.

Jess: Yes.

Momster: How's driving stick going?

Jess: Fine.

Momster: Everything okay?

Jess: YES! Sleepy. Need 2 go 2 bed so I can b alert and drive safely tomorrow. G'Night!

Momster: Okay, okay. Get some rest. Call me when you're leaving in the morning. I love you!

Jess: <3 zzzzzz

Momster: Night night, sleep tight! I miss you!

I'll talk to her longer next time.

- - - - - -

Chunk comes back out, sees me in the driver's seat, and hands me a Slim Jim before settling down on the passenger side.

I readjust the rearview mirror just as his phone swooshes. He looks at it, smiles, and types something. I sigh and pull onto the highway.

Tap tap tap. Swoosh. Rinse. Repeat.

Twenty minutes of nonstop typing later, we pass some dark shapes by the side of the road. They're too big to be horses or cows.

"Are those bison?" I ask.

Chunk doesn't so much as glance away from his screen.

"I don't know."

"You didn't look!"

And then he looks, but of course by then we're past them.

"Who are you texting, anyway?" I hope he reads into my tone that he should be keeping me company instead.

"Lizard from the forum on Penny Arcade."

"Someone you met online?" I can't believe it. "You actually gave him your phone number?"

"Her, not him," Chunk corrects me.

A girl?

"She could be anybody. Anybody! An ax murderer, a pedophile, a con artist!"

"I've known her for a couple of years," he says.

How was I not aware of this?

"You've IM'd with her for a couple of years. That's not the same as knowing someone."

For a smart guy he is really stupid sometimes.

"Never mind," he says.

"No really, think about it! They get your number, they lure you into a dark alley . . ."

Swoosh goes the phone.

"Don't answer that!"

"You're kidding, right?" He's using his Jess-is-stupid voice. "She's my friend! And she's not the only one who has my number."

Chunk's been a member of online forums and chat rooms for years but it never once occurred to me that he considered these people his actual friends. And who is this Lizard person anyway?

I resolve to call her Lizzie Borden.

"Friends are people you do things with."

"Like what?"

He's challenging me.

I try to come up with an example.

"Like talk to, and play video games?" he asks. "Just like you and I do?"

"When you get lured somewhere and ambushed and they

chop off your arms and legs, don't come running to me," I say, staring straight ahead at the road.

"Deal," he says, typing away.

- - - - -

The clock on Betty's dashboard says it's 1:45 when we get to Elko, which according to Chunk's roadside attraction printout is home to White King, the World's Largest Dead Polar Bear.

We won't be dropping in on him tonight.

The task at hand is to find a motel. My jaw aches from the way I have been clenching my teeth at the incoming *swoosh*es emitting from his phone, and the *tap tap tap* of his fingers in reply. I'm glad to have something else to focus on besides Chunk's idiocy in thinking these people he knows from online are friends the same way that we're friends.

We've spoken very little since Winnemucca, but right now he's reading me Yelp reviews of the places we're passing.

We have quite a few choices. I'd pictured tumbleweeds blowing across the road, somehow, but there are businesses and casinos and not a horse-drawn wagon to be seen.

"Surprisingly populated," Chunk observes. The first non–motel-related thing he's said to me in more than an hour.

I nod.

"The word was *populated*."

"Practically cosmopolitan," I say.

"Unexpectedly urban," Chunk says.

"Remarkably metropolitan." I smile.

— — — — — —

Finally we settle on the Red Fox Inn, a squat building just off the interstate. Pretty nondescript, the kind of old-timey motel where you can park in a space right in front of the door to your room. The sign on the roof has a neon fox in one of those old-fashioned nightcaps.

I park next to the office and we get out of the car.

A little bell jingles when we push open the door. The lobby is empty but I can hear the sound of a TV coming from somewhere. We stand there a minute, and finally Chunk calls "Hello?" just as a bored-looking guy with a wispy mustache shuffles out from the other room. He doesn't look much older than we are.

There's a mirror behind the counter, and I can't help it, I check myself out. I know I seem obsessed with mirrors, but I just want to know if I can see what other people see when they look at me.

Right now, I see someone with longish, slightly messy hair, wearing girl jeans and a hoodie sweatshirt. I'm relieved that the stubble I can feel isn't all that obvious.

Chunk steps up to the desk. "I'd like a room."

"Okay," the clerk says, pushing paperwork across the counter for Chunk to fill out. "I'll need a credit card and your ID."

Chunk digs into his pocket to get his wallet and the clerk's eyes slide over to me.

I swear they narrow.

He takes Chunk's ID and studies it like he's working for the TSA or something. Then he hands the card back to Chunk and looks at me. A heat flushes up my neck. His eyes are not friendly.

"I need to see your ID, too," he says.

"But I'm the one paying for the room," Chunk says.

"Policy," the clerk says.

The thing is, I hate my ID. I need to get a new one, and I've started the process, but haven't finished up yet. It'll take a note from my doctor, the ID I have now, and proof that I published my petition for a name change in the paper for a week before I can get my ID gender changed.

I look down. My breasts are safely hidden underneath the heavy sweatshirt.

I take my time removing my driver's license from its plastic sleeve, then pass it over.

The guy looks at it, squints over at me, gives it the TSA treatment, then nods and hands it back.

He runs Chunk's card through the credit card machine and says, "One key or two?"

"One is fine," Chunk says.

Wordlessly the guy takes a key from a row of hooks and tosses it on the counter.

"There's a complimentary continental breakfast from six o'clock to nine." His tone suggests that he's only informing us because he has to, not because he wants to be hospitable.

Chunk takes the key, and on our way out the door I hear, "Have a good night, *boys*."

The room is bland instead of retro kitschy like I'd hoped it would be. For a minute I stand in the middle of it, Space Camp bag in one hand, padded art album in the other. The place smells kind of mildewy, which is odd considering we're in the middle of the desert. Two beds with speckled oatmeal-colored spreads on them sit on beige carpet. A big old boxy TV sits on a brown dresser, and there's a tiny table with a wooden chair on either side of it in the corner.

"Do you think we should push a bed against the door?" I ask when we put down our stuff.

"Why?"

"Didn't he seem weird to you?" I ask.

Chunk pulls his laptop out of its case and sets it on the table.

"Not really," he says.

"What about that thing with my ID?"

"A little strange," Chunk admits. "But maybe he just wanted to make sure you weren't underage or something."

"Or maybe he wanted to know my gender," I say, checking behind the curtain to make sure the window is safety locked.

"I doubt that was it," Chunk says.

"I think it was. I think he could tell I'm trans. This part of the country isn't safe for queer people." My hand wants to smack Chunk for not being more aware of this.

He sighs and plugs in. He sets up his little wireless device.

"What?" I ask.

He doesn't answer right away. He just starts typing. "I doubt he thought anything out of the ordinary."

"You heard him call us 'boys' when we left."

Chunk sighs again and looks at me.

"Your ID still says male," he says, irritated. "I'm sure that's what he was going by."

He goes back to typing and I watch him for a minute. The digital clock between the beds says 2:05.

I want to scream at him for not being more *concerned*. But then I flash on an image of my mom shrieking at my dad when he made a wrong turn and wound up in a scary neighborhood in East Palo Alto, and my dad threatening to put her out of the car.

Yelling at people when you're scared doesn't really make them want to protect you.

"If we want to get to Kearney by midnight tomorrow, we need to leave by eight in the morning" is what I say instead.

Chunk just keeps typing.

"Did you hear me?" I ask, and *oh my God* I hear my mother.

"I heard you," Chunk says without looking up.

"You talking to Lizzie Borden?" I'm channeling my effing mother and I can't stop!

"What are you talking about?"

"You know, your friend." I can't help putting finger quotation marks around the word *friend*. It's like my hands are possessed by my mother, too.

"Are you implying my potential hookup is an ax murderer?" he asks.

"Your potential hookup?"

73

I slump to the bed, and remind myself that she's just someone online. It's not like they've met in real life. And they probably never will. Still . . .

"That sounds like something a frat boy would say," I tell him.

"For your information . . ." He turns the laptop around so I can read what it says. He's typed "TRANS FRIENDLY PLACES TO STAY IN KEARNEY NE" into the search engine.

I stare at the screen for a minute.

"Thank you," I finally mumble.

CHAPTER 7

My neck and shoulders are fused by anxiety from the moment I'm barely conscious. At first the thoughts crowd together in my head, kind of like those cartoons where a bunch of people are trying to get through a door at once, so none actually gets through.

We have to get going. I need to come up with a concrete plan for the wedding. I'm going to show my dad and Jan who I am and I have no idea how they're going to react. Am I really going to wear the Muzzy dress? I should shave. I hate shaving. A redneck clerk insisted on seeing my ID last night. We drive through scary Wyoming today.

Finally one thought squeezes all the way through the door.
Chunk likes a girl named Lizard.

And traveling the distance between Tahoe and Elko, he spent more time texting with her than he did talking to me. My back teeth ache. I can tell I spent the night grinding my molars.

I roll over and grab my phone. It says 8:22. Shit shit shit.

There's a particularly loud snore. I look over at Chunk in the other bed. His eyes are closed and his mouth is open. His hair is a curly black halo. I throw the scratchy oatmeal-colored bedspread off me, and I'm about to rouse him when another thought squeezes through the door in my brain.

He spent a lot of time last night researching trans-friendly places to stay in Nebraska. He was still at it when I fell asleep to the sounds of *Lockup* on the TV.

And I'm torn. I really want to get on the road so we can hit Kearney by midnight. But the thought of Chunk taking his time to find a comfortable place for me, taking his time to make sure I'll be safe, loosens the tension where my neck meets my shoulders by a muscle or two.

I decide that's gotta be worth at least another half hour of sleep for him.

– – – – – – –

He sleeps for another forty minutes or so. I don't take a shower because I don't want to wake him up, so I pass the time quietly drinking motel room coffee, thumbing through my album, and thinking about what palette and materials I would use in a piece that would reflect the memory of this morning.

It would start with color. The puttied shade of the walls as a wash, over the image of a clock, portrait of the artist's contorted face, gazing over at an inert lump in the next bed. Acrylic? Ink?

— — — — — — —

"It's late" is the first thing Chunk says when he wakes up and looks at the time, but he seems unperturbed. He grabs his duffel bag, ambles into the bathroom, and closes the door.

I hear the lock click.

After a monumentally long time, the water for the shower goes on.

I go back to my notes to keep myself from thinking too hard about why he locked the door. He's never done that before.

Maybe I'll paint an outline of the state of Nevada around the figure in the bed.

When Chunk finally emerges from the bathroom fully clothed, his hair is wet, and there's a little curl sticking to his neck. He's wearing his favorite shirt. It has a bunch of ones and zeros on it. He once told me it says "you are stupid" in binary code.

I told him that the gender binary code was even dumber.

Such compatible nerds.

"I'll just jump in and jump out," I say, heading into the bathroom but leaving the door a little ajar.

"I'll go get gas and then come back," he calls, like he can't even be in the next room if I'm in the shower.

He's still gone when I get out. I dry myself, pull on the skinny jeans from the girl side of my closet and a baggy black T-shirt from the guy side that has a few spatters of midnight blue paint down near the bottom.

I imagine a gender clothing continuum for myself, stretching from San Jose (male: baggy sweatshirts and guy's jeans) to Chicago (female: the Muzzy dress and ballet flats).

I brush my hair into a low ponytail, then grab my phone to call my mom. I owe her a longer conversation.

The room is dark, but I don't want to open the blackout curtains. Who knows if the hick clerk is standing outside?

She doesn't answer right away and I start to leave a message. "Hey, Mom, it's me. Just calling to—" The phone picks up.

"Hey, Jess! Is that you?"

"No! It's the Dalai Lama."

"How's it going?" I say just as she asks, "How are you?"

"Fine," we say at the same time, our voices an octave apart.

"How's the trip going?"

"No change since last night."

"And you're really having a good time?" she asks.

"Of course!"

Even though I'm on my way to a confrontation with a transphobic groom. And even though I feel bad that I actually kind of want to see Jan. And even though the biggest reason of all I'm on this trip is to be with Chunk but he's talking to some girl he likes and wants to hook up with. And even though he locked the bathroom door when he took a shower like I was going to jump in and molest him.

"I'm glad you're having fun." She pauses, then says, "Well, hurry back, the house trim misses you!"

I told her I'd help with it after the wedding. This is sort of a compromise since *someone* needs to dig a drainage ditch down the side of the house and that's not a good job for my daintier-by-the-day upper arms. We finally agreed that I'd take care of the house trim and my mom would hire someone to do the ditch.

"I'll lovingly caress it with a paintbrush when I get home," I promise. "So what are you up to today?"

"I thought I'd do some things around here and maybe treat myself to a massage."

"That's all?"

"What do you mean, that's all?" she asks.

"I just mean, isn't there something else to do? Like a lecture at East West or going out to dinner or something?"

"No, just house stuff and a massage."

"You should call Marina and Jeff." Two people she knows from her Spiritual Forgiveness group.

There's a moment of silence. "Are you afraid I'm going to be bored without you?"

"No . . . I just wondered."

Actually I'm worried she might be lonely all by herself in the house.

"Um-hmm. Well, you're very sweet, but I'm fine."

"I wasn't worried."

"Of course not," she says, sarcastic but not mean. "Okay, honey. Let's talk again later. I love you more than anything. Have a good time, and be safe, and don't be anxious about me."

"Love you, too," I say, hanging up.

She knows me so well.

Khaki

8x11 inches

Image: Pyramid of figures wearing Boy Scout uniforms. Portrait of the artist on the bottom row, wearing black stiletto heels.

Pen and ink on paper, watercolor wash

"So, um . . . I think I'm not going to do Scouts this year," I told my parents. I finished the last of my miso soup and set the bowl down on the dining room table. When I was thirteen going on fourteen we had miso a lot because it's what my mom craved. She'd been diagnosed with cancer and had had a lumpectomy in late July. Now it was early September and she was undergoing her second of five rounds of chemo.

I don't think any of us were really worried that she would die. And it'd be going too far to say my dad *hoped* she'd die, even though I once heard my mom accuse him of that.

"Quitting Scouts," he said, stirring his soup. "Is that so?"

It wasn't really a question. He said it in his quiet Dad-menace voice, the one designed to make me back down.

"That's so," I said, holding his gaze, my jaw tight.

I'd saved this conversation for the end of dinner in case I needed to stomp away, because I knew within every fiber of my skinny, almost-fourteen-year-old body that nothing was ever going to make me put on that ugly khaki uniform again.

That week Boy Scouts of America had been in the news because an openly gay scoutmaster had been forced to resign. I planned to cite this evidence of bigotry as my reason for quitting.

At this point I'd come out to Chunk, so he (and his mom) were pretty much the only people who knew. And while I'd wrestled with the thought that my dad wouldn't be completely okay with it, I figured I'd see how he reacted to my quitting for that stated reason, and then go from there.

The timing of the scoutmaster's resignation was convenient in terms of an excuse, but the truth was, there was a pack campout in the Santa Cruz Mountains scheduled for late September, and I was *not* going to go.

Trouble was, my dad was a den leader.

"I don't agree that they made that guy resign," I said, and then held my breath.

"You're just going to walk out on your responsibility?"

My dad put down his spoon.

"How is scouting Jeremy's responsibility?" my mom asked.

I exhaled. My mom was like a cabinet with something nice inside, and when the door was open you could reach in to get it. The trouble was sometimes the door would snap shut, pinching your hand.

The door was open for me right then, and I was grateful.

"Stay out of this." My dad frowned at her.

"And I hate their politics," I said, trying to steer the conversation back to my own agenda.

"No, really," my mom said, putting her spoon down too. "Cleaning his bedroom and making his bed is his responsibility. Taking out the garbage is his responsibility. Not belonging to some club."

"I give up two Tuesday nights a month, and plenty of hours in between, to do Scouts *for him*, and you're just going to let him quit?!"

"And I think their homophobia sucks," I said, to no avail.

"What are you going to do when he wants to drop out of high school?"

"Don't be stupid! This isn't the same thing at all and you know it!"

"You let him quit Little League, you let him quit Pop Warner, and now it's okay for him to quit Scouts!"

"Actually, Dad, I just didn't sign up for Pop Warner again, remember? I was taking that still-life class and . . ."

My mom turned to me. "It's okay for you to quit Scouts, Jeremy. And I agree with you about their homophobia."

"Damn it!" My dad exploded. "You're constantly undermining me!"

"When you're being an idiot!"

And they were off.

I don't know why I'd thought for a second that I could make any conversation happen the way I wanted it to, not even when it involved me directly. No one stopped me when I picked up my dishes, carried them into the kitchen, and listened to the rest of the argument from there.

"Why is it you let him walk away from everything? Especially activities that are a chance for us to bond?"

"Because the *activities* that you want to bond over are asinine! And he has no fucking interest in them! Try bonding with him over something *he's* interested in! Forcing him to do stupid macho stuff like football and Scouts is never, ever going to make him a masculine kid! That's just not going to happen because he is who he is. And you're stupid to think you can make him straight!"

"I'm not trying to make him anything, and even if he *is* gay, letting him quit everything is bad for his character." But my dad's voice lacked the force it had had just twenty seconds before.

Relief flushed through me. Just as I had known in my bones that I was done with Scouts, I rejoiced that there didn't seem to be a need to have a big, dramatic coming-out-gay scene with my parents.

I'm not sure what made my dad back down from trying to make me stay in Scouts. Maybe he was listening to my mom for once in his life.

In any case, he made a point of sticking to his commitment as den leader for the rest of the year, though on the Tuesday nights of the month he didn't go to the meetings, he instituted a father-son movie night.

He always let me choose what we were going to see, and I always made a point of picking romantic comedies or else the classic films shown at the Stanford just to see him frown. Which he did, but he never complained.

So maybe some of it really was about bonding with his gay kid.

CHAPTER 8

Chunk finally gets back from filling up the car with gas, and he's in a hurry to get on the road. I check my reflection again. I'm probably okay without shaving until tomorrow.

When we get in, the clock on Betty the Car's dashboard says 9:55.

"Breakfast?" I ask.

He shakes his head. "We'll stop in a little while."

I tear open the snack-size bag of Doritos and offer some to Chunk.

"Nah, I'm good."

I shove a handful in my mouth before grabbing my sketchbook and pulling the list of roadside attractions out of the glove compartment. I look down to see what there is in Utah.

In the margin, next to the Iowa attractions, Chunk's penciled in *Riverside, Iowa*. It wasn't on the list yesterday.

"What's in Riverside?"

Chunk adjusts the sideview mirror before answering.

"The Future Birthplace of Captain James T. Kirk. We can't pass *that* up!"

I have my doubts about this, but whatever.

A huge camper passes us. The words *Land Yacht* are painted in gold and black on the rear panel.

"We should have bought a land yacht," Chunk says.

"Then we could sleep in it!" I agree.

"And put a Jacuzzi in the back," he says.

"And pick up a hitchhiking marching band."

"And some cattle."

"To feed the band," I say.

"It takes a lot to feed those guys," Chunk agrees.

"No kidding." I laugh. "Have you seen the size of their tuba player?"

How much do I love our nonsensical conversations? I'm sure they're better than any he's ever had with Lizard Borden. I grin over at Chunk but he's changing lanes and too focused on the road to notice.

— — — — —

A half hour later, the hotel room coffee is gnawing at my stomach. "Aren't you starving?" I ask.

Chunk's eyes are glued to the road. "Nuh-uh," he says, just as his stomach growls like some . . . growling beast thing.

"Wait a minute! Did you eat when you went to get gas?"

"No." His voice is peeved. "Why?"

"Because I'm effing starving, so you must be too."

"Why would you assume that?" he asks.

I think about it. "I just meant dinner was a long time ago, and I ate all the Doritos and . . . and now I'm hungry, so I figured that you must be, too . . ." I trail off. Why does he sound so weird?

"If *you're* hungry, then we can stop," he says. "Just don't assume that we're stopping because I want to eat."

"Fine, *I'm* hungry. Can we please stop?"

But of course on this stretch of I-80 there's nothing but a carful of silence eventually broken by the sight of Metaphor: the Tree of Utah on the horizon.

Metaphor: the Tree of Utah is on our list of roadside attractions. It's an eighty-seven-foot-tall fake tree. The giant trunk is a deep beige color, and I count six huge greenish spheres attached to different points along it. I guess those are supposed to represent the leaves. A few segments that look like someone cut apart a mammoth tennis ball lie scattered on the ground at the base. The whole thing looks like it was constructed by demented space aliens.

We don't stop; no one can. There's a fence with razor wire around it to make sure no one gets too close. We pass it going almost sixty-eight miles per hour, which is huge for Betty, but not as fast as the cars around us.

It's like everyone wants to get away from the sight as fast as possible.

"I'm trying to figure out what Metaphor is a metaphor for," Chunk muses.

I turn on the camera.

"Captain's Log, Stardate 11706.15. First mate discerns that

86

Metaphor: the Tree of Utah is a metaphor for ugly-ass art surrounded by a chain-link fence with razor wire on top."

"Good one, but the captain believes the first mate has metaphor confused with example."

And I don't mind that Chunk's correcting me in that way he does, because it feels more normal now. And he's kind of smiling.

I decide not to worry about his weirdness in locking the bathroom door, or even Lizzie Borden. Chunk's just being stupid. It's not like they're ever going to meet.

- - - - - - -

Utah is full of beauty and wonder and mountains for skiing and trees to look at. Or so I've heard. An hour and a half later, the reality of where we are is this: variegated shades of brown and tan and desert nothingness.

There's been nothing to draw for eons, and I'm sorry for my neglected sketchbook. I doodle a green gecko so it won't feel like I'm ignoring it.

Even the hum of Betty's tires on the pavement *feels* brown and empty. It's hard to believe pioneers crossed this void on horseback. It must have taken them forever. Even in a fast car—okay, a fast car relative to a horse—I feel like there's nothing ahead of us and nothing behind. A glance at the speedometer tells me we're going sixty-five. The speed limit is eighty.

"Maybe the desert is a brown hole," I say. "Kind of like a black hole but it sucks you in slower."

Chunk nods. "I can see that."

"Or, maybe it's just us going slower," I say, turning on the camera.

"Captain's Log, Stardate 11706.15. Must find planet with beryllium to give Ol' Betty a boost."

"Starship Betty is getting you to Chicago, first mate. Shut your piehole," Chunk says.

"Mmmm, piehole. I'd choose that over black hole any day," I say, turning off the camera and pulling out my phone.

I type in "electrolysis New York."

$125.00 an hour seems to be the going rate.

"This blows," I mutter.

Chunk fumbles with one hand to turn on the camera.

"Captain's Log, Stardate 11706.15. First mate disgusted by scenic view of sector Utah."

"No, I mean how expensive it is to get rid of this." I rub my jaw. "I'm going to look like Wooly Willy for the rest of my life unless I win the lottery."

Shaving's just another one of those shitty things. I have to do it, because I don't want to walk around like the bearded lady. And it sucks.

Chunk turns the camera off. "Trivial Pursuit?" he asks.

"What's the capital of Tanzania?" For some reason this is the first question to come to mind.

"Dodoma."

"The thing about shaving is, it feels so masculine, you know?" I say.

"Gotcha," Chunk says. "You don't have to go into it."

For once he's not trying to get me to share my feelings, and I'm not sure how I feel about that.

His phone *whoosh*es and his eyes flicker toward it.

How much is it torturing him not to break his own rule about cell phones in the car?

— — — — — — —

It's well after noon and we're about a half hour from Salt Lake City itself. I'm so hungry I could chew the upholstery out of Betty. Still, we have to stop at the Great Salt Lake before we look for food so we can check it off the list.

Chunk pulls into a viewing area off of I-80. The odor of sulfur combined with the smell of rotting flesh assaults my nose even before we open the doors. My appetite disappears.

"We could bottle the smell and use it as an appetite suppressant." I gag.

Chunk takes the camera off the dash and we get out to take a look. The water's pretty far away from where we are, and the beach, which was supposed to be salt-white, is mottled with black gnats and dead birds. Dozens of them.

"What the hell?" I ask.

"Look up dead birds and Salt Lake," he orders, already filming the putrid scene.

I google it on my phone and am immediately rewarded. "Avian cholera. It looks like it happens a lot here, and isn't dangerous to humans."

Chunk continues to film. "Captain's Log, Stardate 11706.15.

Planet Great Salt Lake is hereby demoted to Planet Fetid Lake."

"It is the opinion of the first mate that Planet Fetid Lake has nothing to offer but the heebie-jeebies," I say, and am rewarded with a half smile from behind the camera.

"That's a wrap," Chunk says, and we get back into Betty.

Ten minutes later we take an exit that has a little blue sign of a gas pump and underneath that a knife and a fork and a plate, indicating a restaurant.

"It'd be great if the sign showed chopsticks and a takeout carton of Chinese, too."

"The knife and fork *are* kind of ethnocentric," Chunk agrees. "But maybe there's just no Chinese food here."

Which is true, of course. In fact, there are only three buildings off this exit: a gas station, a convenience store, and a restaurant with a peaked roof and brown slab-stone walls.

We pull into the parking lot of the Three Bears Diner and get out of the car.

At the entrance a huge figure of Goldilocks holds an empty bowl that was presumably recently full of porridge. She's round and satisfied looking.

"My God, it looks like she ate Baby Bear," I say when we walk past it.

Chunk says nothing until we slide into the red vinyl booth and the waitress comes around. Then he asks if they're still serving breakfast.

"Sure are, hon. We serve it twenty-four by seven."

"Great. I'll have the oatmeal," he says, sliding back out of the booth. Before I can raise my eyebrows at his choice, he says, "Restroom?"

She points him in the direction of the two doors at the back of the restaurant. One says Momma Bear and has a cut-out picture of a bear in an apron. The other says Poppa Bear; Poppa Bear is smoking a pipe.

Gender stereotypes aside, I kind of like it that Smokey Bear evidently has a brother who went bad.

"What'll you have, miss?" the waitress asks.

I smile and order something called the Three Pigs: eggs, ham, bacon, and sausage.

When the waitress leaves, I take a look around. The only other customers are a couple sitting in a booth across the room. There's definitely a children's storybook theme going on in here. On the wall next to me are two paintings. One is of an extremely worried-looking Humpty Dumpty. The egg part of him is gargantuan, but he has tiny little hands, one of which brandishes a blue handkerchief to wipe the sweat off his brow.

The other painting is Little Red Riding Hood, happily skipping through the forest, while the wolf leans up against a tree watching her. He's standing on his hind legs, and something about his posture screams juvenile delinquent. I fight the urge to grab a Sharpie and give him a cigarette dangling out of his mouth.

When Chunk gets back from the bathroom I lean across the table toward him.

"She called me 'miss'!"

He doesn't respond, and I feel stupid for telling him, like I'm bragging or something. I get that pinchy feeling behind my eyes, and I'm glad when the food arrives so there's something to focus on.

Chunk eats his oatmeal with gusto. When the pinchyness dissipates, I offer him a piece of my sausage (no jokes here). He turns it down and picks up his phone.

I finish my food to the sound of dishes clattering in the kitchen and the *swoosh* and *tap* of him ignoring me.

— — — — — —

After a half hour on the road with little to no conversation, I'm reading from the trivia app on my phone while Chunk drives. We're going through Salt Lake City now, and it looks pretty much like any other city. Right after we left the diner Chunk announced that the Mormon Tabernacle—which I wanted to drive by because the photos I've seen of it are beautiful—was a sight, yes, but not a roadside attraction, and if we had a hope of reaching Kearney tonight there was no way we could see it.

It wasn't a discussion. He's being weird so I let it drop.

"'Category, Geography. What are the meat-filled dumplings of Mongolia called?'"

"Wait! What was that?" Chunk says, and I look up from the screen.

"What was what?"

"That sign that said I-15."

"As in interstate?"

"Yes!"

"Did you take an exit you didn't mean to take?" I ask.

"No!" Chunk snaps.

The GPS isn't on because really, how hard should it have been to stay on 80?

"Well, something must have happened if we're on the completely wrong road." I can't keep the accusation out of my voice.

I shut down trivia to turn on the GPS, but it's uncooperative. *"I'm sorry, I am unable to connect at this time."*

"We'll get off here and I'll figure it out." Chunk sighs, like it's my fault somehow.

He takes the next exit and there's nowhere to pull over at first, but a block later we park on the street, between two corrugated tin buildings with graffiti on them. He turns Betty off and grabs his phone.

ZOLO says one tag in red spray paint. Another says HOLD'N in silver and purple.

At first the GPS on Chunk's phone isn't any more cooperative with him than mine was for me.

I jiggle my leg.

"We're fine," Chunk says.

"I didn't say anything!"

There are only two other cars in sight. In the distance the sound of a bass pulses over the noise of freeway traffic, but I can't see where it's coming from. Somebody's scrawled COP KILLER in foot-high black Sharpie on the cinder-block wall across the street.

I point. "Are there gangs in Salt Lake City?"

Chunk looks up from his phone and shrugs.

The air-conditioning turned off when we stopped. It's warm, but I don't want to roll down the window.

"Directions to Interstate 80," Chunk says twice more before the voice of his GPS says, *"Getting directions to Interstate 80 East, Salt Lake City."* And then, *"Proceed two hundred feet. Take onramp to Interstate 15 South."*

Chunk squints down at the screen, perplexed. "I don't know how we could have gotten off 80."

He enlarges the map, and pushes it this way and that for a minute.

The difference between me and Mr. Going-to-Stanford is that I don't care how we got lost, just that we did.

Getting unlost and out of this neighborhood takes precedence over figuring out the how and why of it. "Never mind, let's just go."

"Oh . . . mystery solved." His voice is sheepish. "80 becomes 15 for a while."

Chunk starts Betty and my stomach unclenches a little. We pull out and follow the directions back onto the freeway.

"Well, *that* was smart," I say.

Chunk frowns and I do too.

Once again I have just channeled my pre-enlightened mother.

Copper
10x13 inches
   Image: Witch's hat next to broken broom.
   Background, concrete wall tagged with graffiti.

Portrait of the artist confined within one of the cinder-block squares.
Wooden frame inlaid with 99 pennies.
Acrylic, wood, pennies

The long national nightmare that was my parents' marriage finally ended in the fall of my freshman year of high school.

The last thing we ever did as a family was to go see an art show that some of Jan's students were having at a community center in Palo Alto.

My parents drank wine and ate cheese and crackers. Mom had had her last chemo in August; it was now November and her tests indicated that there were no cancer cells playing house in her body.

So she was, you know . . . free to abuse it with alcohol and fat.

I wandered around the converted multipurpose room looking at art with Jan. Most of it was pretty unremarkable, but I was happy just to be with her. She hadn't been around much lately since my mom had gotten better—not that I blamed her for that. For some reason, post-treatment, my mom had been even more disagreeable. No one could do anything right, not even Jan.

I loved that when Jan introduced me to the students and other art types who came up to her, she always followed the introduction with "Jeremy himself is a remarkable artist." With that praise, coming from the Silicon Valley Museum's assistant curator, people would look at me differently, like a person instead of a kid.

At the end of the night my parents came over to where Jan and I stood, discussing a twenty-inch sculpture, one of the few standout pieces of the show.

Thousands of hammered pennies shined to a brilliant copper rose up from a base into two figures. One, a featureless male, slogged forward, his shoulders sloped. Weary, determined. The other, a female figure rising up from a solid mass of pennies, arms wrapped around the male's legs, as if trying to pull him back down. The female figure had a face; penny scraps formed sharp eyebrows. Lips parted in a shrieking howl. Its title was *Pennies from Hell.*

"I like that the male doesn't have a face," I'd said just as my parents came up.

"Me too," Jan said. "It's as though he's the Anyman."

My mom glanced at the piece, but her gaze didn't linger. "It's ugly."

Jan got her art instructor hat on. "What makes it ugly to you?" she asked.

My mom was having none of it. "I don't have to analyze every little thing. It's perfectly valid to say I find something ugly." Her voice carried. I was mortified.

"Shhhh!" my dad said, glancing around to see if anyone overheard.

No one was looking in our direction. People were still sipping wine and checking out other pieces.

"What? I'm entitled to my opinion!" But she lowered her voice. "I just don't like it."

Jan nodded coolly. "Enlightening critique." She and my

dad exchanged a meaningful glance. Sort of an isn't-Mary-being-a-bitch thing.

My mom caught the look, and there was a brief and awkward silence while she glared at her best friend of twenty years.

"Well, thanks for inviting us," my dad finally said. The party was clearly over.

Jan leaned in to hug me. "I'm so glad you came, Jeremy." I squeezed her back, she and my parents hugged, arms stiff, and then we left.

"That was tacky," my dad said once we were in the car headed home.

"Tacky? How is expressing my opinion tacky?" my mom snapped.

"Mom, the artist could have been standing right behind you!"

She turned around to frown at me in the backseat.

"Artists have to learn to take critique sometime."

"That wasn't a critique, that was an uninformed opinion!" my dad said, speeding up to get around a silver Prius.

"So now I'm stupid?"

And once again they were off into a bickering argument that ranged from art to my dad's neglect of my mom when she'd been sick.

I texted Chunk.

Me: Still okay to come over 2nite?
Chunk: Yup. Bring Mordock's Giant.
Me: Duh.

(We were both addicted to the game at that point.)

A very long time after we should have been on the freeway there was a break in the argument.

"Where *are* we?" my mom asked.

I looked up to see an unfamiliar residential area. Doors and windows had black bars over them, and chain-link fences surrounded yards that were just scrabbly patches of grass and dirt.

Ahead there was a cinder-block wall tagged with the letters *E.P.A.*

"Oh my God! Are we in East Palo Alto?" My mom's voice was edged with hysteria. I scrunched down in the backseat. At the time, East Palo Alto was known for crime and gang violence.

"Shit," my dad said, steering the car down one graffiti-covered street after another, trying to get turned around so we could go back the way we came. The trouble was, there were one-way streets to contend with.

At each stoplight, when other cars pulled up next to us, I held my breath and was careful not to look directly at the people driving them.

The whole time my mom was yelling at my dad to "turn here, don't go down there, my God, don't go that way!"

My dad, increasingly flustered, drove down a street with no outlet.

"Well, *that* was smart." My mom's voice was so mean.

We got to the dead end of the street and Dad turned the car around slowly, watched by three tough-looking guys in baggy jeans and sideways baseball caps. Two of them were smoking, and the other just stared, an unfriendly expression on his face.

"You IDIOT!" she yelled at my dad.

We were two dilapidated houses away from the end of the street when he slammed on the brakes and turned to my mother.

"I will put you out here if you don't Shut. The. Fuck. Up."

Their eyes locked and hatred shimmered in the air. This was beyond bickering and I *knew* my dad meant it. If my mother uttered a single syllable he would force her out of the car.

I looked back at the end of the street. Nonsmoker had left his friends behind and was heading toward us.

I watched his approach, biting the inside of my cheek so hard the taste of rust filled my mouth.

"Dad, please?"

My voice broke their death stare. Mom swallowed and looked away.

My dad nodded once and then stepped on the gas. Silence crushed the inside of the car and we eventually found our way back to the 101 freeway.

I escaped to Chunk's as soon as we got home.

By noon the next day, my dad's closet was empty.

CHAPTER 9

The mountains on the other side of Salt Lake City are mostly brown, but then trees start to dot the landscape here and there. We've been quiet, listening to the soundtrack from *The Avengers* since I channeled my pre-enlightened mom.

So far Wyoming looks nothing like the desolate vista I'd imagined. I turn my sketchbook to a fresh page.

"I'd expected it to look more . . . Road Runner–ish," says Chunk, the old-timey cartoon addict.

I know what he's talking about. Those cartoons had a kind of open, flat feel to them . . . Nothing like what we're taking in. Another image that comes to mind is from *The Laramie Project*, the play we did my sophomore year. It's based on the true story of Matthew Shepard, a gay college student who was beaten and left to die. I'd researched it a little for the set design, and my research had shown miles of flat landscape, a desolation and ugliness so intense it made you want to cry and give up on life just looking at it. Of course, my research was only on the Laramie area of Wyoming, and that's a ways from here.

"There's plenty of ugly up ahead," I say.

"That's why we should enjoy this," Chunk says.

I look over. He's right. The trees are pretty, the sky is vast, and sometimes it's nice to enjoy beauty while you can.

There's a billboard for Little America, advertising seventy-five-cent ice cream cones.

"It's on the list," I tell Chunk. He shakes his head no.

"Captain's Log, Stardate 11706.15. Captain hostile to ice cream."

"Isn't Little America the place with the dead penguin?" he asks.

"Yep."

"I think we can skip it," Chunk says. "We missed the world's largest dead polar bear too, so there's a kind of symmetry. We're ignoring animals from both the poles."

"No ice cream?"

"Do *you* want ice cream, Jess?"

I'm still full from breakfast. "Not really."

"Me neither." He addresses the road ahead. "I'm eating a little differently these days."

"Duh," I say. "Oatmeal."

"It was nasty," he concedes.

"We don't have to eat ice cream, you know. What if we stop but don't have any?"

"We'll see."

"Game?" I ask.

Chunk nods.

I put down my phone, grab his, and unlock the screen. He's received three texts we didn't hear over the sound of the road and the music. I pull up the Truth app without mentioning them.

The first question isn't too great. "'Does food automatically taste better when you cook it yourself or when someone else does? Why? Describe the perfect meal.'" I thumb through to find a better one.

"Oh, here's a good one."

"Is this Trivial Pursuit?" he asks.

"'What physical traits do you find most attractive? Would you date someone if they lacked the physical but had personality traits that really jibed with yours?'"

"I thought we were going to play Trivial Pursuit," Chunk says.

"I know. Tell you what, let's answer this one, and then we'll change."

"Let's change now."

"No, let's answer this question now."

"Do you want to tell me what *you* find attractive, Jess?"

"No, I'm more curious about what you like. What's your type?"

I'm not sure I believe in types, but incredibly enough, this is something we've never talked about.

I look over. Chunk's eyes are on the road.

"C'mon. Tell me."

He shakes his head.

"Why don't you want to tell me?"

He changes lanes.

"Because you're just going to use what I say against me."
A Porsche roars around us.

"No I won't. I'm just curious."

"I think you will."

"How?" My voice jumps an octave, and in spite of my irritation, I can't help but be a little pleased with the sound.

"I just feel like no matter what I say, you're going to point out all the ways Lizard doesn't have whatever traits I say I find attractive when you meet her. I mean *if*," Chunk says quickly.

"Like that's ever going to happen."

He's on his own when it comes to meeting ax murderers from the Internet.

"I know she's not trans or gender queer or anything to do with you . . . so you're not interested."

"Huh?"

"Never mind." He downshifts. "So . . . traits I find attractive."

"Go back. What do you mean I'm only interested in people who are trans? Are you saying I'm only interested in people like me?" Ham and bacon and sausage expand in my stomach and I'm a little nauseated.

Chunk doesn't say anything for a minute. I'm staring at him. He taps his fingers on the steering wheel and then says, "It's not all the time, but I'd say very often it's about you. We're always talking about *your* feelings. What you like, what you don't like."

I can't believe what I'm hearing. "That's because you're always asking me!"

"Right. And when, unless it was in a game of Truth, have you ever actually asked me anything about *me*?"

I think for a minute. "I think Truth should count."

He shakes his head. "Those aren't real questions coming from *your* curiosity."

A huge burgundy van passes us. Someone has written "Go Wyoming Waves" in shoe polish on the back window.

"I've told you about Lizard, for instance, and you don't seem interested at all, except as something to make fun of."

"She's just some girl you met on the Internet!"

"I've known her for a long time and there's a chance we could hook up—something big for me."

"What the hell?"

"Forget it," he says.

But now I need to know more. Like how he's planning to hook up with someone he's never met in person, and where does she live?

"I'm sorry. Please tell me about Lizard." I put down his phone, turn my sketchbook back over, and look down at my gecko.

"Never mind, Jess."

"No, really. I'm sorry. Where does she live?"

"A killer smile," he says.

I give the gecko a clown mouth with razor-sharp teeth.

"Lizzie Borden has a killer smile?" I add blood to the teeth.

"I'm going back to traits I find attractive. I don't want to talk about Lizard. You've been weird ever since I told you about her."

"You've been weird since before that!" Even as I say this, I know it's true. I feel like it started after Mrs. Harris thought we were a couple. My stomach really hurts now.

Chunk doesn't respond except to turn on the radio.

We listen to excruciating Christian rock for the next fifteen miles or so.

When I can't stand it anymore, I turn it off.

"Fine. So you like killer smiles. Anything else?"

He sighs. "Look, I don't know. I just said that."

"Why would you just say that?"

He takes his hand off the gearshift and scratches the back of his neck. "Truthfully? I have no idea what physical traits I'm most attracted to. I'm a guy who deals more in mental and emotional traits."

"So, what mental and emotional traits do you find most fascinating?" I ask.

"An intelligent person who demonstrates an interest in my life," he says.

And even though the landscape is whizzing by us, the air in the car goes very still. There's an uncomfortable minute, and then the sign for Flaming Gorge comes up.

We say "Flaming Engorged" at the same time, then laugh and laugh in that immature way you do only with the best friend you've had forever.

- - - - - - -

Forty minutes later and the billboards advertising Little America just don't stop. At first they say things like ARE WE THERE YET?, LITTLE AMERICA, and PLAY LITTLE AMERICA with a picture of a couple of golfers from the waist down. Then there's 7 MILES TO 75-CENT ICE CREAM and a few minutes later ALMOST THERE.

By the time we're a mile from the exit, an ad showing a line of penguins shaking their tail feathers melts Chunk's resistance.

"We can top off the tank. I'm not getting ice cream, though," he tells me. We pull off the exit and drive toward a ginormous gas station that's to the right of a long, low red brick building.

I don't know what I expected, but it turns out Little America is mostly a truck stop, with a motel and a gift shop attached. The advertised golf course and kick line of penguins are not immediately evident, although there is a penguin statue on the roof of the combination motel and gift shop.

"We'll get gas, go in, check out the dead penguin, and be on our way," I assure him.

I've never seen so many gas pumps in one place. Ever. And I've never seen so many big rigs and cars lined up to get gas either. There must be fifteen fuel islands, each with two pumps. And at every one of them there's a vehicle fueling.

The big rigs are in a section to the left. We drive toward an area a short distance from them, where people driving regular cars are getting gas. It's crowded, but no one seems to mind. There's almost a carnival atmosphere.

It's sort of like people are thinking, *Hey, we made it to the oasis that is Little America after a hundred miles of nothing! Who cares that it turned out to be a truck stop?*

Chunk drives up behind a black Volkswagen Jetta that's just pulling away from the gas pump.

"I'll get this one," I say, reaching behind me and unzipping my Space Camp bag for my wallet.

"Naw, I got it. We're just topping her off. You can buy next time," Chunk says, stopping the car and taking the key from the ignition. He opens his door, and immediately we're assaulted by the heat and the odor of diesel. It must be ninety degrees.

He takes an exaggerated breath. "Ahh, the smell of freedom . . . or of fossil fuel . . . or whatever it is we're always fighting about in the Middle East."

He shuts the door. I reach into the snack bag at my feet and grab a Dr Pepper.

I sip it and survey the cars around us. A lot of families in minivans and SUVs. The back window of the green sedan ahead of us has a bunch of bumper stickers from places like Mercer Caverns, Mount Rushmore, the Bonnie and Clyde Ambush Museum, and the Corn Palace. I even spy a yellow Mystery Spot, Santa Cruz, CA sticker. The glut of bumper stickers on that car tells me those people probably didn't get suckered.

They came here on purpose.

It's getting hot in the car and I open my door to a beeping noise coming from the pump. I look through the back window at Chunk, who grimaces.

"The card reader's broken. I have to pay inside." He hikes off across the pavement to the cashier.

I pull down the rearview mirror to check my reflection, see no visible stubble, and get out to wash the bugs off the windshield.

When I pull the squeegee out of its little bucket, the soapy water looks pretty dirty. I shrug, step to the driver's side, and start scrubbing. Gray water and bugs smear across the glass.

The white SUV on the other side of the pump drives off, a blue Honda Insight just like Betty pulls up, and the driver gets out.

He's in his early twenties, I'd say, sun-bleached-blond surfer-dude hair, a square jaw, wearing a pink T-shirt that says MAKING A RUN FOR IT: BREAST CANCER AWARENESS 5K. I can't help but notice he's pretty muscular. Not in a gross weightlifter sort of way, just like he cares about physical fitness or something.

Evidently the card reader over there is working because he manages to start fueling right away. He clicks the handle into place, looks over, notices Betty, and smiles.

"Excellent taste in vehicles," he says.

"Thanks."

"What year?"

"Um? I'm not sure." Still scrubbing at the dead bugs with the squeegee, I casually use my other hand to slide the elastic band off my low ponytail so I can shake my hair into my face a little.

"Looks like 2006. I think that was the last year they made the two-door."

"Oh, I didn't know that. Neat." I don't know what's neat about it, actually. Am I passing?

"Sorry." Surfer Dude's smile is toothy, genuine. "I'm a total nerd about these cars, and you don't see 'em too often."

I turn the tool over so the black rubber part can scrape off the goo. "They're cool, right? Get fifty-six miles to the gallon, not too imagey, and the insurance is cheaper because it's an older model," I babble in Chunk-speak, then turn the sponge side down again. I stretch out, trying to reach a spot in the middle of the windshield where a giant splatter is visible.

"Exactly! Now if only they came with bug-resistant windshields," he says.

The insect that created that splotch must have been made of Super Glue, and I'm having a hard time in part because my arm is short, and with the squeegee extended, I can't exert pressure downward.

"Here, let me help you," Surfer Dude says, coming around the front of the car.

I take a step back.

"Oh, you don't have to, I've got it." Does my voice sound okay?

"No trouble," he says. "I need to do mine, too."

I hand him the squeegee, keeping my face slightly averted. Then I look down at my filthy palm.

"There's paper towels over there." He points to a dispenser near the bug water.

I walk over to grab one, conscious of his eyes on me. The towels are fibrous and blue; they'd make good absorbent material for blotting watercolor. I grab a few extra.

"You local?" he asks, expertly scrubbing and swiping.

"There's nothing around here for eighty miles," I say, wiping my hand. "I don't think anyone is local."

He nods. "You're right. The employees probably all commute by helicopter." I lift my head and smile at him. Who *is* this guy?

Chunk comes back just as my hero scrapes the last bug corpse off.

"Jess?"

Surfer Dude looks over. "Hey, man," he says, giving one last swipe. "She was having trouble reaching a spot."

She!

"Thanks," Chunk says. It's a dismissal.

On the other side of the pump there's the telltale click of the gas shutting off.

Surfer Dude retreats to wash his own windshield.

"He's a fellow Insight enthusiast," I tell Chunk.

"Huh," he says, unscrewing Betty's gas cap and sticking the nozzle in.

The friendly vibe of a minute ago is completely broken.

Surfer Dude gets in his car and gives me a surreptitious little wave as he drives off. Can he see my apologetic smile?

When we get back into Betty I say, "I would've thought that you guys would've bonded over your love of the Insight."

Chunk pulls away from the pump. "Meh."

"What do you mean, meh?"

"He looked like a jock," he says.

"I thought he looked more like a surfer."

Chunk reaches up to readjust the rearview mirror. "Why was he washing Betty's windshield?"

"I was having trouble doing the middle. Oh, I get it! You're jealous!"

"That's stupid."

I glance over and Chunk's shoulders are so stiff they're practically up by his ears. Does he think I'm serious?

"Because no one but you is allowed to touch Betty."

His shoulders relax and he smiles. "Hey, when you have a hot babe . . ."

"Yeah, but he had one just like her," I say.

"Maybe he was one of those guys who fantasizes about twins," Chunk says.

"Maybe," I agree.

Chunk finds a place to park.

"Ice cream's starting to sound good," I say.

"Not to me," Chunk says just as a bead of sweat rolls down his temple. "I could use a cold drink, though." He grabs the camera and gets out of Betty.

We cross the baking asphalt toward the restaurant and gift shop. Over the top of the building, near where the penguin statue is perched, a yellow helium balloon floats up to the sky. We pause to watch it from the sidewalk.

"Heartbreaking." I mean it. "When I'm rich I'm going to buy a truck and fill it with helium tanks and go around to fairs and circuses and everyplace balloons are sold just waiting for a kid to lose theirs, so I can replace it."

"That's really cool!" Chunk exclaims. "And in the unlikely

event you don't get rich, I'll fund the venture, and we can do it together."

On the grassy area in front of the building there's a life-size bronze buffalo, and a cartoony looking green brontosaurus the size of a fat horse. Two little kids are climbing on it, and their mom's taking pictures. Across the grass another family sits on a gray metal bench eating drippy seventy-five-cent ice cream cones.

We push through the doors into the air-conditioned haven. To our immediate left there's an incredibly crowded gift shop and to our right an incredibly long line for ice cream. We forge ahead, following arrowed signs pointing to HOTEL REGISTRATION and EMPEROR THE PENGUIN.

We find him in the motel lobby, standing inside a glass case. He's a couple of feet tall, and wears that dapper look penguins do.

A sign on the wall next to the case tells us that Little America was conceived of by an S. M. Covey, a shepherd who wanted to create a way station for travelers in this desolate part of Wyoming, because he'd once spent a freezing night outside in the area. He arranged to have a live penguin shipped over to be the mascot. Of course the penguin died before he made it, so poor old Emperor was stuffed and put on display instead.

"Did it really not occur to anyone that the change in temperature was going to kill him?" Chunk asks.

"What I want to know is, do you think he left behind a little penguin family? Is there some widow penguin who mourned for the rest of her days because her husband was taken away? Or was she glad to get rid of him?"

"Probably neither one," Chunk says. "A lot of penguin species mate for life, but not the emperor penguin."

I take the camera from him. "Captain's Log, Stardate 11706.15. First mate has advice for avian species of planet Little America. If you're a penguin, you're probably not going to find a penguin that's any better than the one you've already mated with. No point in trading in one for the other."

Chunk nods. "That's a wrap."

On the way out the lines for food and beverages are still too long, and we forgo even a cold drink in favor of getting on the road. Back in Betty with Chunk at the wheel, I sip warm Dr Pepper, thinking about Mr. and Mrs. Penguin. If my dad were one, he'd definitely be of the emperor variety.

Orange
10x16 inches
>   Figure of a woman clad in a towel, eyes wide, mouth puckered. Three-headed dog nips at bottom of towel. Portrait of the artist opening the gates of Hell.
>   Oil on canvas

The background noise of a streetsweeper humming down the road filled my ears. I stood in front of the garage at my dad's condo, frustrated, trying to remember the key code to get in.

Dad's new place was a few blocks from the house, which was supposed to make my life easier for the one-week-here/one-week-there arrangement my parents had settled on.

The arrangement itself was a pain in the ass since it

seemed like whatever I needed was never at whichever house I was staying in at the time.

That May there was a poster contest at school for freshmen. It was a Mom-house week, but of course my tempera paints were at my dad's. School had been a half day. I'd gotten out at 12:17, and here I was trying to get into Dad's without my keys, which were, of course, at my mom's.

On the third try a little flash went off in my head, and I punched in 007. The garage door rumbled up. I hoped that burglars didn't know my dad was a James Bond fan.

He was supposed to be at work, but his garage wasn't empty.

The minute I saw Jan's Verde Chiaro Fiat, I *knew*.

She'd been unavailable pretty much from when my dad moved out, six months before. When it first happened she came over and listened to my mom bitch about how she was sure my dad was going to screw her in the divorce, but then Jan just kind of disappeared.

And we hadn't had a Saturday art date in a long time.

I stormed past the Fiat and slammed through the condo until I found her in the kitchen, wearing a tangerine bath towel. It was from the set my dad had taken when he left.

As soon as she saw me, she clutched her coffee mug and her face went blank. Like she just couldn't compute.

"Let me guess, the shower at your house is broken?" I spat out the words.

Her expression changed momentarily, like she thought she'd found an excuse, but I didn't give her a chance to lie.

114

"Tell my dad hi." I turned to leave. "I'll tell my mom you said hi, too."

She was supposed to be my mom's friend.

"Jeremy, wait!"

"Screw you!" She was supposed to be *my* friend.

Paints forgotten, I ran home, *I hate you I hate you I hate you* pumping in my ears.

The phone was ringing when I charged in the front door. Mom was in the living room, and from the kitchen where the phone was, caller ID kicked in.

"Call from Jan Nelson."

"Don't answer that!" I shouted from the foyer, thundering on my way to unplug it.

Mom followed me.

"Jeremy, what's wrong? Are you okay?"

My heart pumped betrayal and hatred, but my mom actually sounded . . . frightened.

I turned toward her to tell her I was fine, but couldn't.

"Honey?" Warm arms around me, hands patting me. Her hair was still super short, but soft and downy against my cheek. I was a few inches taller than her.

"Jan's over at Dad's," I said into the top of her head. "In a towel."

She stiffened for just a second and then went on patting me, but the pats became more mechanical by the time I pulled away.

Her skin was translucent gray, like it had been during the worst of the chemo, and her eyes focused on something in the distance.

"Mom, are you okay?"

She didn't respond right away.

I led her to the couch and we sat with our arms around each other like we were sole survivors of a tornado.

She finally spoke. "That *bitch*!"

And that was all she would say for the next several minutes. Over and over and over, like a mantra. I cycled between hatred for Jan and my dad and a growing fear that my mom was having some kind of nervous breakdown. Where would I live? What would I do if she had to be hospitalized? Would the Kefalas take me in? Living with the man who caused this would be out of the question.

I was on the verge of calling Chunk's mother for help when my mom snapped out of it. It was weirdly abrupt. One minute she was chanting and the next she was giving me a squeeze and saying, "Well, *that* was surprising."

I didn't know whether she was referring to Jan being with my dad, or her own reaction. But then she said, "I'm okay now. I'm okay. Are you okay?" I was so relieved I could only nod yes.

— — — — — — — —

The next day my dad came over when my mom was at work. He tried to explain, but it just made me more furious. He and Jan had abandoned my mom, but I wasn't about to. I didn't care what the custody arrangement said; from then on I'd live full-time with my mom. And I let him know that if he ever brought up Jan, I wouldn't see him at all.

I meant it and he knew I meant it.

After that, I made sure our visits dwindled to nothing more than an uncomfortable meal or a movie once a month.

Jan herself called and called and called. She tried to grab me as I was leaving school one day. I was on the tech crew for the spring musical and she showed up to a performance. I ignored her.

Five months after I caught them, she got the position of curator for the Chicago Modern Museum. My dad left his job at Genentech and took one at DuPont to move with her. Most of me was glad to see them go.

The rest of me couldn't believe they had given up so quickly.

CHAPTER 10

I always thought "the sky opened and it poured rain" was just an expression, but that was before witnessing what I am right now.

Chunk slows down.

A summer storm could be a fine thing, I'm sure. When viewed from a wrap-around porch on a day when you have nothing else in the world to do. But just now, an hour or so after Little America, and when Kearney tonight is starting to look like a long shot, a summer storm does not seem like a fine thing at all.

I check out the speedometer. Not only are we barely going fifty miles an hour, I need to pee. Damn Dr Pepper.

There doesn't appear to be any easy place to stop and I don't really want to be the one holding us up by having to go out of our way.

I lean over and look at the gas gauge.

"Um, do we want to top it off again?" I ask.

Chunk turns into this used-car salesman, so happy is he

with the great mileage we're getting. "Nope, I estimate we won't need gas until sometime next year," he says.

"Oh . . ." I let it trail off. I consider how much longer I can wait. Not much, I decide. "The thing is, I kinda need to pee."

"Why didn't you say so? There was a sign back there that said there's a rest stop up here somewhere."

I didn't see it. "How far?" I ask.

Chunk's phone swooshes and I swear the sound pierces my bladder.

"Um, thirty miles, I think?"

I mentally calculate. We're now going forty-nine miles an hour. The clock is ticking and my bladder is full. Actually, if my bladder were a lifeboat, it would be throwing people to the sharks right now.

I have never been the kind that could pee into a bottle, or even just pee with someone standing next to me at a urinal.

I'm about to tell Chunk he just needs to pull off the road and I'll do my best to hide behind the car, when I see a sign up ahead. Chunk slows down and we read it: GAS STATION AND MEL'S FAMOUS PASTRIES: 5 MILES.

"Thank God," I say.

Chunk starts singing. "Raindrops keep falling on my head."

"Stop it."

"Just around the riverbend . . ."

"Knock it off."

"The water is wide . . ."

"Please stop?"

"Okay, okay."

We exit the highway and follow the arrowed signs to a red-and-white building with two gas pumps. Chunk starts to pull up in front when I see a sign with another arrow that points around to the back of the building. The sign says ES-TROOMS because the *R* is missing.

I can see lights on inside the building, but the place looks pretty deserted.

"Just drive straight back," I tell him.

"What if we need a key?"

"If that turns out to be the case, you can go ask for it, and I will relieve myself on the side of the building," I inform him.

I get out of the car, and as I'm closing the door, I notice a rusted shovel leaning against the building. It's ominous. Like it's there for the purposes of victim-burying or something.

By now it's raining so hard my head is drenched in just the few steps it takes to get from the car to the building.

I pull my T-shirt loose on my body, hunch my shoulders, and try the door that has the male symbol. It's unlocked. I look over my shoulder. Should have shaved this morning. I choose the men's room in case anyone is there when I come out.

The place is surprisingly clean and there's an air freshener that smells like pink bubblegum.

I pass the urinal, go into the stall, and sit down to use the toilet. It's the most wonderful thing in the world, feeling all the pee leave my bladder. Even the thought of the rusty shovel outside can't take away from this smallest human pleasure.

I swear I have an almost zen moment. Worries about Chunk and Lizard, or getting to the wedding, or what I'm going to say to my dad to make him see me as a girl, or whether Jan will be happy to see me, all just slip away in the physical relief I'm experiencing. And for the first time, I kind of get Chunk's whole human bathroom experience.

Of course my moment of zen only lasts for as long as it takes to relieve myself, because I catch sight of myself in the mirror washing my hands. My hair is plastered to my head, I swear I can see scalp underneath, which makes me worry about premature balding, and despite the budding breasts that are obvious in this shirt when I stand up straight with my shoulders back, I think my face has never looked more male.

I hate the way I look right now.

I turn away from the mirror, throw open the door, and get ready to dash out to the car, but the car's not there.

What was Chunk thinking moving it? I peek my head around the corner and see the car now parked on the other side of the building. Why would Chunk leave me to walk so far back to the car? It's raining buckets! And doesn't he know there are rednecks in this part of the country?

I inch my way down the building.

I know Chunk thinks I'm paranoid, but there's a good reason, right?

He's not in the car, and the doors are locked. I hunch next to it, rain falling on my head, trying to make myself small and unnoticeable. Through the rain I stare at the parking lot entrance, willing all other cars to stay away. The fact that they do isn't really decreasing my anxiety, though.

I picture the headlines. *Trans Teen Found Tortured and Killed in Nowheresville, Wyoming.*

Chunk finally comes out of the building.

"Let's go! Let's go!" I say, my hand on the car door handle waiting for him to unlock it with the remote. I'm careful to wait for the beep, though, because I don't want to waste time with that thing where you lift the handle too soon, and the beep hasn't sounded, so the car doesn't unlock and there's that whole shifting around trying to synchronize with the person unlocking and the one holding the handle.

I don't hear the beep. I look over at Chunk. He's standing there with a huge smile on his face, oblivious to the fact that fat raindrops are bouncing off the lid of the coffee cup in his hand.

"You've got to come in! I want to show you something."

"I wanna get gone, before someone puts my head on a pike, or whatever it is they do to queer people here," I say.

"Trust me, you *have* to see this," Chunk says. "It'll be okay, I promise."

"This is worth me risking bodily harm for?" I ask.

"You'll be fine, really."

I can see he is not going to let this one go.

"Let me get my sweatshirt," I say.

He unlocks the car and I lean in. It's awkward because I'm wet but I manage to get it on while bent into the car from the waist.

"I want you to know you're the one who's going to have to explain to my mom what happened to me," I say, straightening up.

"Relax," he says, and turns to go back into the store. I follow him, making a mental note to steal his extra key and keep it on me at all times to avoid this scenario in the future.

Even in the rain, the window front of the store catches some light and gleams. When we step through the door there's a musical *ting*, like a fairy has just waved a wand.

I look around at the typical convenience store displays. Gum and motor oil and toothpaste, all items that wouldn't be next to one another in a regular store, but here it's like it's the Wild West of product stocking.

Toward the back of the store, there's a glass display case with pastries in it and I become aware of the smell of vanilla and apples. It smells like a French bakery, not like a convenience store named Mel's in the middle of nowhere. "Did you forget something?" a gravelly, smoked-cigarettes-for-fifty-years voice asks from behind a curtain at the back of the store.

An extremely tall figure with bright red hair and peach-colored lipstick emerges, holding a tray with turnovers on it. The figure crosses to the counter behind the glass case and sets the tray down next to an honest-to-God shotgun. Taking her hands off the tray, she allows one to rest meaningfully next to the gun.

"Um, just wanted to see if you had any . . . fat-free . . . stuff," Chunk says like he's been caught doing something.

I'm focused on the shotgun.

"These just came out of the oven," cigarette voice woman says. "Not fat-free, though. Nothing here is."

"They smell great," Chunk says, moving closer to the back of the store, whereas I'm the type to walk *away* from people with guns, not toward them.

But then I notice something as arresting as the gun and much more welcome. This woman has an Adam's apple. I almost put my hand up to touch my own.

I exchange a glance with Chunk. This was what he wanted to show me.

I swallow. "We'll take two, please," I say, stepping closer and fishing some money out of my damp pocket.

The sight of money seems to convince her to step away from the gun for a moment as she reaches over and grabs a little white bag for the pastries.

Chunk steps forward and grabs a couple of apples from the basket on the counter. He holds his coffee cup between his arm and his body and transfers both apples to one hand while he struggles to get his wallet out with the other.

"I got it," I tell him.

"We'll take the apples, too." I look down to see a pack of bubble gum in a rack. "And this." I put it on the counter.

The woman nods and moves over to the cash register. I allow my sweatshirt to lie flat against my body.

"Are you Mel?"

Which is stupid, because her name kind of doesn't matter; what I want is to ask other questions, like *How do you live here, and when did you transition? Did you always know, or did you figure it out later? Do you ever worry everyone's going to think you did it just because you're a cross-dresser, not because you really felt misery in your birth-sex assignment?*

"That's me," she says. When I hand her the money, she gets a look at me, a good look, and her eyes meet mine. I can't say there's exactly some flicker of recognition that passes, nothing so obvious as that, but she does count back my change slowly, then she asks, "Where are you all headed?"

"Illinois," Chunk answers.

Mel nods once, and then looks directly at me again.

"You be careful."

And that's it.

We walk back out to the car.

"And you were worried about Wyoming!" Chunk says.

"Mm-hmm," I say. I think of the me in the mirror washing my hands in the bathroom, not brave enough to claim the women's room. Worried about whether I pass, and what people think.

Here is Mel, so effing brave in this definitely gay-unfriendly place. She's made a life for herself. Or maybe just managed to keep one.

Brave, brave, brave.

Then I remember she has a shotgun, and I do not.

And *then* I remember that the woman with the shotgun warned me to be careful.

I turn on the camera. "Captain's Log, Stardate 11706.15.

Friendly native of desolate planet Wyoming has warned us to keep shields in place."

"I think she just meant don't be obvious." Chunk checks the rearview mirror before pulling back onto the road.

The rain lets up, and we haven't gone very far when we see an honest-to-God rainbow. I thrust my head out the window and shout to it. "If you're gonna stick around here you better protect yourself! You're being too obvious! Lose a little color, whydontcha?"

Chunk and I laugh, but I imagine Mel getting up in the morning, putting on peach lipstick and having to grab a shotgun for safety, and my heart hurts a little.

It's hard enough for people like me and Mel to be who we are.

Silver
10x14

Image: Portrait of the artist as a young woman in a frame of silver eyeliner pencils. Glitter heaped in the lower left-hand corner.
Acrylic, pencils, glitter

My hand shook the first time I put on eyeliner. I had to dab it off with a Q-tip and then start over. It was my sophomore year and I'd been roped into designing the makeup for the Kennedy drama club's production of *A Midsummer Night's Dream*.

I sat on my futon surrounded by compacts and brushes and intriguing pots of makeup, pretty stoked by the assignment. The summer before my freshman year, before she became Jan the Evil, Jan had taken me to see a theater-in-the-park version of the show. I recalled there being a lot of saturated colors and glitter involved. My plan wasn't to copy what I'd seen exactly.

I knew I wanted even more glitter in my design.

I'd sketched out the makeup of Titania, the Queen of the Fairies, and now in the privacy of my bedroom I was using myself as a model. I propped a little hand mirror on the dresser and I could only see part of my face at a time, which was great for making sure all the little details were right before checking out the full effect.

After finally managing matching silvery-black upstrokes at the outer corners of both my eyes, I outlined my lips with a blood-red pencil from my Ben Nye makeup kit. Next I filled in the fleshier part of my lips with magenta lipstick.

I chanted in my head, *It's just for the play.*

But the chant couldn't drown out a deep thrum that started the moment I'd opened the kit and persisted in my belly even as I picked up the tiny mirror, studying pieces of my face.

Arched eyebrow here, rouged cheek there.

The insistent vibration grew when I put down the little mirror and headed into the bathroom. I flipped a switch, and the room went from black to light.

I looked toward the mirror.

A girl stared back at me, and the thrum in my torso exploded with joy and recognition.

In that moment I *knew* what I was.

This was about something much bigger than my body; my soul was undeniably female.

I touched a finger to my bottom lip, knowing in that moment that even without mascara, blush, foundation, and lipstick, I was, and always had been, a girl.

So many things clicked.

The cringe every time my dad had called me "big guy." Why my skin itself felt stretched in ways it shouldn't have been. Why, when I fantasized about sex with a guy—I'd never done anything with anyone—his body played a much bigger role in the fantasy than my own did. I fantasized about touching a guy, but not the other way around.

For just a moment the molecules that made up my body buzzed with a joyous knowledge that what was between my legs didn't mean I had to see myself as a guy. I took a step back from the mirror to see my entire reflection.

Immediately on the heels of the ecstatic flush and buzz came the hideous realization that my penis *did* make me a guy in the eyes of everyone else.

And that it always would.

I didn't get out of bed the next morning.

– – – – – –

We've been back on the road for about thirty miles when I lean down to grab a bottle of water from the floor, and the seat belt pulls tight across my upper body. It's a little painful. I sit up and open the bottle.

"I keep forgetting how sensitive they are," I say to Chunk.

He grunts. I pat my chest gently. My new breasts feel like the skin is stretched over something a little spongy, almost.

"Gotta love those hormones." I try to say it in a sarcastic tone but I can't keep the pleased note out of my voice.

"I know. Keep your eye out for mile marker 184," he says, just as we come to a sign that says CONTINENTAL DIVIDE ROAD ½ MILE.

When we get to the exit Chunk says, "What do you call a divide that needs Depends?"

"I have no idea."

"An *in*continental divide!"

"Your grandpa called, he wants his joke back."

Chunk doesn't care. He's smiling as he unhooks the camera from the dash and opens the door. We both get out of Betty.

Not only has the sky cleared, but the sun is beating down pretty hard for six p.m., if you ask me. The rain clouds are completely gone, replaced by nothing more than a heavenly royal blue, like a picture postcard.

We stand looking out on a vast horizon that actually is starting to resemble the Wyoming of my Laramie Project research.

Sorry, Wyoming, despite your amazing sky, there still isn't anything I want to sketch here . . .

I turn to Chunk, water bottle in hand. "What gives? I was going to pour it out so half would flow to the Pacific and half to the Atlantic. But there's not even a hill here."

Chunk turns on the camera, and in his professor voice he

says, "That's not how it works in this place. We're actually standing in a unique spot along a divide that's over three thousand miles long, the Great Divide Basin. Which when you think about it is pretty cool in and of itself."

"Not as cool as being able to pour my water out and watch it run in two different directions."

"No! It is." Chunk sweeps the viewfinder left and right—capturing what, I don't know. "I read about it. We're standing in an endorheic basin."

This means nothing to me.

"The word was *endorheic*."

"Synonyms? Really?" I make a big show of punching myself in the arm so he doesn't have to. "I have no idea what that word means."

"The fact that it's endorheic means nothing flows to the Pacific or the Atlantic. Water here does its own thing, unlike almost every other place along the Continental Divide."

I ponder this for a minute. I consider my stubborn facial hair and my sensitive breasts, and then crouch down and pour half my water onto the earth at my feet. It briefly pools and then soaks in, leaving a faintly darker patch of brown.

I stand up and toast the entire basin with what's left in the bottle.

"You know, I'm doing my own thing too. Here's to us."

Chunk continues filming and I'm waiting for him to make a Captain's Log, Stardate statement.

Instead he says, "Wow! Way to make even a geological phenomenon about you, Jess."

"What?"

"Just kidding." He turns off the camera and gets back into Betty.

I get in, too. He *was* kidding, right?

CHAPTER 11

Just after eight o'clock we grab food from the Subway off of I-80 near Laramie.

I make Chunk go in alone while I wait in Betty. When he's gone I remember to grab the extra key he has tucked under the floor mat and slide it into my pocket.

He rolls his eyes when he comes back with his hands full and I have to unlock the door from the inside. The parking lot's dead but I'm taking no chances in this part of the world.

Chunk inhales his sandwich while we're still parked so he can drive.

"You've been driving all day. Are you sure you don't want me to?"

"I'm good. Maybe in a little while."

"What'd you get?"

"Turkey, no cheese." He digs into the sunflower seeds from yesterday.

My meatball sandwich smells amazing. I haven't even taken a bite yet. I want to savor it.

We pull back onto 80, and I feel sorry for him. Poor guy must still be starving.

"Want half?" I ask.

"Naw," he says.

I take a huge bite. "It's really good," I say from around a mouthful of sauce and meat and toasty Parmesan bread.

"Maybe just a bite," he says, keeping his face forward but leaning toward me, his mouth open. I hold up the sandwich so he can have some. Feeding him feels oddly, stomach-twitchingly intimate. When he takes a bite his top lip brushes my knuckle.

My flesh prickles and he jerks up straight again, eyes never leaving the road.

Did he feel it too?

I grab my phone in one hand and open the trivia app to stave off a weird silence.

I read questions out loud and eat my sandwich during his answers.

— — — — —

At almost nine o'clock, the sun's gone down behind us, but it's not dark yet. We're approaching what Chunk's printout tells us is Buford, Wyoming's Tree in the Rock.

There's just enough light to see, and I read the description on Chunk's printout aloud.

This limber pine has been around so long that when the railroad was built in 1867, the workers jogged the track

sideways to avoid it. The railroad was eventually moved
south, and the stretch was paved as Lincoln Highway.
When Highway 80 was built, the tree was again left alone,
the highway splitting around it.

"Isn't the Two-Story Outhouse around here too?" Chunk
asks, exiting into the center median, just as a Volkswagen van
pulls out of it, going in the opposite direction.

I check the list.

"Yeah, but it's a little off the highway. Maybe we shouldn't
bother with stuff that isn't right on 80?"

"Except for Riverside," Chunk says, parking.

"I don't get your sudden interest in the Future Birthplace
of Captain Kirk."

"I just think it'll be cool."

"Whatever."

Chunk grabs the camera. We get out, stretch, and walk
closer to take a look at this tree, which indeed seems to be
growing out of a boulder. There's a tall and stabby-looking
fence surrounding both tree and rock.

I take the camera from Chunk and turn it on. It's getting
dark and we probably won't be able to see much.

"Captain's Log, Stardate 11706.15. Citizens of Planet Wyoming fear tree and rock will escape, have built enclosure to
keep that from happening."

"Yeah, as if the cement shoes weren't enough," Chunk
agrees, pointing to the stone base.

I turn off the camera and he hands me the keys. "You can
drive."

– – – – – – –

Which of course means that we're back to *tap tap swoosh*. I check out the time and realize that there's no way we're going to make it to Kearney before at least two in the morning. I don't know if I can stand Chunk's Lizard-fest that long. Also, somehow we're spending less time hanging out in cozy motels and watching bad TV on this trip than I'd envisioned.

I cheer myself by thinking about how much more time we'll have coming home after my dad's rejected me. And maybe Chunk'll be sick of the reptile by then?

"We're getting into Kearney super late."

"Yeah, but I figured it out already. We can stay in Ogallala." Chunk says the name of the town in the weird Fozzy Bear voice I haven't heard him do since we were in sixth grade.

It makes me smile.

"That's a place?" The very name Ogallala demands to be said in Muppet dialect. "Are there queer-friendly motels in *Ogallala*?" I ask, using my Fozzy Bear voice, too.

Chunk's quiet for second. "No."

"So we should keep driving and stay somewhere else, right?"

"No . . . ," he says.

I glance over and he's looking intently out the window. "Maybe I just wasn't using the right search terms, but I couldn't find any trans-friendly places to stay in Nebraska at all."

I swallow.

"We'll be fine," he says. "Remember, we'll arrive and leave under the cover of darkness . . . and you pass better than you think you do. Plus I'll sit on anyone who even looks sideways at you."

It's rare for Chunk to make a fat joke about himself, and I don't know if I'm supposed to laugh. But his mom has a saying: *The meaning of the message is the response that it elicits.* Which means pay attention to the message behind the words.

Chunk is saying he'll keep me safe.

"Thank you."

He nods once, and gratitude surges, making me teary in a good way.

It starts with gratitude for having Chunk as a friend, that he'll be by my side when I confront my dad. The feeling morphs and seeps through, to include gratitude that I hung in there. My life is so much better than it was two years ago.

Black
24x24 inches
   Image: Computer monitor showing portrait of the
   artist being sucked into space.
   Acrylic on wood

Trying to sleep at night was miserable once I realized who I really was, and I spent hours online instead. A famous athlete had come out, and "transgender" was all over the media. The realization that that word, with its sharp prefix "trans" and mumbly suffix "gender," most likely applied to me gave me no comfort.

I didn't bother with homework or gaming or drawing. Instead the darkest hours were for obsessively googling.

Transgender. Transsexual. Transvestite.

and

Gender queer. Gender fluid. Gender variant. Gender dysphoria.

I slogged through a gut-twisting amount of trans hate and fetishism to find information. What I learned mostly was to stay away from the online comments section for anything having to do with gender nonconformity.

One night I came across an interview with a couple of trans teenagers that originally ran on the TV show *20/20*, and also a show about a trans seven-year-old whose family supported her. I watched them over and over before downloading them to a folder on my desktop and going back to googling.

After my nightly search-fest I'd lie sideways on my futon and stare out through open curtains into the inky black of the night, never managing to fall asleep much before the sky began to lighten. As soon as my alarm went off, I'd will myself back to sleep, hoping to at least dream I was in the right body.

It took about a week for my mom to notice I'd stopped doing pretty much anything including shaving and bathing.

I'd drag myself to school and then come home and take a nap. My hair got stringy and wisps of facial hair scraggled in. I looked awful, but I couldn't rouse myself to do anything about it.

At least once a day Mom'd poke her head into my room. "Are you sure you're okay, Jeremy?"

"I told you, I'm just exhausted," I'd say to the woman who'd endured months of chemotherapy.

Mondays sucked the worst. The weekend hours might have been filled with nothing but an endless and obsessive stream of thoughts about my body and my life, but the thought of going to school and seeing the girls who were born that way tortured me even worse.

Why them?

Why me?

I avoided Chunk, who assumed I was busy with the play, when in reality I was so far behind in the makeup design that my dragging trail through the school building included an exhausting, out-of-the-way arc just to avoid the wing that housed the drama club.

On the third Monday I tried to stay home, my mom came into my room and sat down on the edge of the futon. I pressed myself against the back folded part, trapped because she was sitting on top of the sheet.

This was before she'd gone all zen. Her eyes were concerned, but her mouth was exasperated. She'd had enough.

"Listen, mister. Either you're going to tell me what's

bothering you or you're going to get up and get your ass to school."

In the year since my dad and Jan had abandoned us, we'd gotten a lot closer, but confiding in her was still taking some getting used to.

On that morning I was exhausted beyond caring what she might think.

I struggled up and out from under the sheet, grabbed my laptop from my desk, clicked open the folder of trans kid videos, and angled the screen so she could see it.

I watched her face as she watched the first segment. Eyebrows scrunched together, lips parted, she absorbed what was going on with those kids. I knew my heart was pumping because I could hear its rush in my ears, but the rest of me felt outside of my body.

Before the first clip even ended, she turned toward me.

"You?" was all she said.

I nodded, the word *yes* caught in my throat.

Her forehead smoothed, she took the computer from me and put it on the floor. Thin arms pulled me onto her lap like I was little.

"My baby, my Jeremy."

I burst into tears and she did too.

I cried with exhaustion and the knowledge that even though she knew, it didn't change the facts. I was a girl with the body of a guy.

We sobbed and rocked and rocked and sobbed until we were both spent. Finally I said, "I really, really need to pee," and we both laughed that shaky laugh you laugh when you've been crying for what seems like forever.

She released me, but before I could stand, she grabbed my face with both her hands and kissed my nose. Then she said the weirdest thing.

"I was so afraid you were missing *them.*"

CHAPTER 12

It's really dark now. I made Chunk play trivia with me as a way to keep his constant conversation with Lizzie Borden at bay, and now my arm is tired of being punched. I'm calling Black Hole before Chunk can even get the questions out, and we're a little . . . well . . . punchy.

About twenty miles outside of Ogallala there's a rest stop, and Chunk wants me to turn off so he can use the bathroom.

"Way to keep me safe," I tell him.

"You're fine. It's late, and no one is going to be there anyway."

"Picture the headlines," I say, even as I'm slowing to take the exit. "Recent High School Graduates Found Decapitated in the Hatchback of Honda Insight on Lonely Highway."

Chunk shakes his head. "I'm pretty sure the headline'd read something more like, 'Valedictorian Christophe Kefala and Unnamed Friend Found Drowned in Honda Insight: Kefala's Mighty Bladder to Blame.'"

"Dude, that's just gross."

"I know, I know! That's why we need to stop."

I pull into the parking lot of the squat building.

There's one other vehicle in the lot, a pickup truck, and it's sitting at an angle, facing away from the building and illuminated by the powerful security lights in the lot.

I find a space as far from it as possible.

"You're fine," Chunk says again when he sees me eyeing the truck. I become aware that I also kind of need to pee, but now I'm not getting out of the car.

The pickup is one of those awful behemoths—it sits up on giant wheels that belong on a city bus. The kind that I doubt is driven by anyone who is friendly to your garden-variety queer person. There's what looks like a shark fin on the top of the cab. The back window is tinted so you can't see in, but I imagine a gun rack in there. A couple is standing outside of it, engaged in what looks to be tense conversation. Chunk gets out of Betty.

"Be right back," he says.

"I'll be right here," I say, and lean over, lowering my voice. "Unless those two are zombies, in which case, you're on your own." Chunk saunters over to the building and I lock the doors. Come to think of it, zombies might be preferable to rednecks.

I decide they're not zombies when I hear the girl say, "I don't even care! I just want you to stop acting like I'm too stupid to know!"

If they were zombies it'd sound more like *guuuurrrrr-rrrrrraaaahhhhh.*

I scrunch down in the seat and angle the rearview mirror to the side so I can watch them.

They look like they're around my age. The guy is really tall and skinny with a crew cut that'd make a marine proud. The girl only comes up to the guy's chest, and her hair is a red not found in nature.

It's as though all the deep magenta lipsticks in the world have been melted together and used as a palette for her hair dye. It's cut asymmetrically, so that one side slants across her pale cheek, like a bird's wing. She's wearing a fitted jacket with a zipper that angles across her front, like it's mimicking her hair.

"I didn't say you're stupid!"

"No, you just act like I am!" She throws down her cigarette and grinds it under her boot. "I'm done talking about this. Let's go."

God, her boots.

They are the most awesome boots I've ever seen in my life. They're close to the lipstick red of her hair, and even though they aren't cowboy boots, they have cowboy bling on them, little spurs in the back just above the chunky heel.

Those boots are made for walking, grinding out cigarettes, and maybe kicking ass.

The guy must know this, because he acquiesces immediately. They climb up into opposite sides of the cab and peel out of the lot, shark fin on top glowing, tires squealing.

I listen hard after it disappears down the road until all I hear is the low hum of insects in the warm air.

I think about the girl's clothes and picture myself in a fitted jacket with skinny jeans tucked into cool boots. I add a fringy scarf and smile. Maybe someday my style won't be a no-style style.

When Chunk gets back from the bathroom he says, "They went screaming away! I heard it from inside."

"The zombies are restless tonight." I get out of Betty and head into the women's room.

Come August, maybe I'll even dye my hair.

When I get back to the car, Chunk is talking on the phone. Visions of quirkily fashionable me are replaced by visions of no-style me smacking Chunk.

The texting with Lizard was bad enough. Does he think he's just going to cozily chat away while I drive?

I get in on the driver's side and he makes an uh-oh face. "Oops," he mouths.

I yank on my seat belt. I'll show Chunk peeling out!

"I'm sorry, Ma!"

Ma?

Oh.

God, I feel stupid. And relieved. But mostly stupid.

I don't start the car.

I have *got* to stop with the jealousy.

"There's a drought. I know, I know," he says into the phone. "I'm sorry."

There's more mom-noise, but it seems to be the wrapping-it-up kind.

I make up a new mantra. *Bitchy and jealous be gone. Bitchy and jealous be gone.*

"Yeah, Ogallala. Uh-huh. We'll be safe. Uh-huh. She's okay," he says, turning to smile at me. He mouths, "My mom says hi."

Chunk just called me "she" to his mom.

WTF?

I get out of Betty, slam the door, and stalk to the other side of the parking lot.

For the second time in sixty seconds I want to commit violence against Chunk. It's not just that I don't want to have to put up with his mom's prying (although that's huge), it's that I *trusted* him. He promised to keep my transition to himself until after I left for school.

Gut twisting, I bend over, hands on knees.

I hear him get out of the car.

"Jess, are you okay?" His voice is soft. I'm breathing hard, too angry with him to speak.

"Jess?" His voice is closer and I feel a warm hand on my back.

I stiffen but say nothing. He takes his hand away. "We left the hose on. Mrs. Harris called because it flooded the yard and started running into the street."

I look up at him.

"You called me 'she' to your mom!"

He blinks. "No I didn't."

"Yes you did! I heard you!" I stand up straight. "You said, 'Uh-huh, we'll be safe. She's fine.'"

"I'm sure I said he."

"You didn't!"

"Look, I'm sorry if I did, but *if* I did, she didn't say anything about it, so relax."

As if. I stomp back over to Betty and he follows.

"You drive," I say in the nastiest voice imaginable.

Chunk silently takes the driver's seat. I slam the passenger door when I get in.

He *promised.*

Brown

14x22 inches

    Image: Empty yellow lifeboat drowning in sea of candy bar wrappers in the foreground. Portrait of the artist in top left corner.

    Acrylic, ink, candy wrappers

The whistle and hum of the Mario Kart theme assaulted my ears. The controller was heavy in my hands, and my thumbs felt clumsy.

Chunk sat next to me on the floor of my bedroom, empty Snickers wrappers littering the orange-and-brown rug.

It was now or never.

It'd been five months since I'd told my mom, and I'd been seeing a psychiatrist almost every Monday afternoon since then.

Dr. E was a specialist in gender identity my mom found through an online group that helps trans people and their families. At our first meeting he told me he wasn't there to "cure" me, just to support me while I figured things out for myself.

I could have done that with a psychologist, too, but my mom went straight for someone who could prescribe antidepressants because I needed them. I was still miserable, jealous of girls who were born with girl parts, unhappy in my own skin, and tortured by puberty, because I didn't realize the truth about myself until it was too late for puberty blockers.

There were times that the only bright spot in the week was getting to go talk to Dr. E.

Gradually, though, things did get a little better. Not great, but better. I started doing my homework again, and sketching, and gaming with Chunk.

After talking about it a lot with Dr. E, I'd decided to come out to Chunk.

He was cool with me being gay, but I worried about telling him I was trans. What if it was too freaky for him?

Or what if he didn't believe me? Like what if he thought I was making it up, or it wasn't real somehow because I wasn't one of those people who just knew from the get-go they'd been assigned the wrong gender?

Dr. E had pointed out that I wasn't responsible for what other people thought about me.

But that didn't mean it wasn't going to hurt when I found out what they did think.

More and more, though, it seemed like I was lying to Chunk by not telling him. He knew I was depressed but didn't know why.

I leaned forward and turned off the game.

"Dude! I was winning!" Chunk's mouth opened; his eyebrows were outraged. "What the heck?"

"I have to tell you something," I said.

The March wind howled around the outside of the house, and my gut swirled with it.

I'd role-played this conversation with Dr. E, imagining different scenarios, but in the face of the real thing, all the carefully chosen words blew away. I bit the inside of my cheek.

"I'm a girl. I was born with guy parts, but I'm a girl."

Usually Chunk's silence before reacting to things didn't make me nervous. He'd always been a think-before-you-speak kind of guy, but just then every millisecond he didn't speak was like someone piling another heavy stone on my chest.

When it felt like the rocks weighed more than my whole body, I couldn't stand it anymore.

"That's-why-I've-been-going-to-see-a-psychiatrist-I've-been-figuring-stuff-out-and-he's-been-helping-me-and-I-thought-you-should-know," I babbled, then stopped.

He looked down at the graveyard of Snickers wrappers and slowly nodded.

"Does your mom know?"

"Yes."

"Your dad?"

My gut started to settle. Chunk hadn't yet run from the room screaming.

"No."

I planned to tell him the next month when I visited Chicago over spring break. The thought of it scared me even more than telling Chunk had.

"Are you going to have surgery?"

Dr. E and I talked a lot about gender being about more than body parts. Still, he warned me that the surgery question was one of the first things people were going to ask, and that it was okay to tell them to mind their own business.

But I wasn't going to say that to Chunk.

"I don't know. Not now."

He nodded like he got it, then he stood up and said, "I'll be right back."

He walked across the hall into the bathroom and shut the door. I heard the overhead fan go on and the swirling in my gut returned with a vengeance.

I focused on tearing the Snickers wrappers into smaller and smaller pieces.

What was he thinking in there?

When he finally came back out, I'd shredded wrappers until the pieces themselves were too small to shred further.

He sat down next to me and picked up his controller. "Do you want to be Yoshi or Princess Peach?"

The swirling gut slowed a little. Was this his way of telling me we were cool?

"Are you okay with this?"

"I'm fine, you're a girl. It's all good," he said, sounding almost dismissive.

"Are you sure?"

He turned toward me. Our eyes locked. His weren't freaked out . . . just serious. "I'm sure," he insisted and then turned back toward the screen.

"Yoshi or Princess Peach?"

"You can't tell anyone, all right? Not even your mom."
Especially not his mom.

"Duh."

"Promise."

"I promise I will tell no one." He reached over and turned the game back on.

- - - - - - -

The next time I went to his house there was a book called *Transgender Explained for Those Who Are Not* on his desk.

"I grabbed it from my mom's study," he said when he saw me noticing it.

I panicked. "But you didn't tell her about me, right?"

"Of course not," he said.

And I believed him.

Like an idiot.

CHAPTER 13

Chunk's been in the driver's seat for at least ten minutes when he says, quietly, "I'm sorry."

I've been sitting with my back against the door and my arms folded across my chest since the rest stop thinking, *Even if he thinks she didn't catch it, I just want him to apologize for slipping up. Just say sorry, just say sorry, just say sorry.* But when he does I can't just say, *It's okay.*

I do shift my body so I'm looking out the windshield rather than glaring at him.

"You should be more careful when you talk about me to your mom."

Up ahead an orange-and-yellow caution sign blinks. I think it's an Amber Alert at first, but when we get closer it says CONSTRUCTION ON 80, DETOUR ON FRONTAGE ROAD NEXT 15 MILES.

"I'm *sorry*," he says again.

I sigh and pull up a game of Truth, keeping an eye on the road at the same time.

Concrete barriers line the sides and narrow the divided highway into a two-lane road for the next two hundred yards, and then a metal gate thing forces us off the highway onto a smaller road that runs mostly parallel to the highway. It's late and there are very few vehicles out and about, yet we somehow manage to wind up behind an eighteen-wheeler.

I read the question, "'Would you cheat on a test if you knew you wouldn't get caught?'"

Chunk doesn't have to think even for a second. "Of course not."

"You don't need to," I say.

"Yeah," he says. "But people cheated off of me all the time."

I'm surprised—I hadn't known that. From the time we hit Kennedy we rarely ever had classes together unless they were in the general curriculum, like health and driver's ed. Otherwise his were all AP and mine were all . . . Normal P.

"And you let them?"

Chunk makes a weird huffing noise. "It's not like I had a choice."

He adjusts the rearview mirror, then says, "I don't think Brian Candless would have passed tenth grade if it weren't for me."

"Brian Candless? I didn't know you were friends with him!"

Chunk looks away from the road at me like he can't believe what he's hearing.

"I wasn't!"

"So why did you let him cheat?"

"Do you really not remember how he used to . . . harrass me?"

152

"When?"

"Oh my God, Jess! The entire freshman and sophomore years!"

"He was an asshole to everyone," I say, thinking back. Thank God he moved to Texas after tenth grade. We should've sent the state a sympathy card when that happened.

"Not like he was to me—I can't believe you don't remember this!" The vehemence in Chunk's voice surprises me. "He got the whole class to chant 'Chunk with the junk in his trunk' every time we had to do anything in PE!"

"I never had PE with you," I point out.

"You don't remember how he used to sing the baby elephant walk every time he saw me?"

"He was just an asshole."

"Jesus, Jess! He *bullied* me. And now you're telling me you never noticed?"

"I'm sorry! He was a dick to me, too."

I'd seen him do that limp-wrist gesture thing when I walked by a couple of times. It was shitty, but I wouldn't say he bullied me.

"Incredible," Chunk mutters.

"What? I'm sorry!" My apology's defensive, even to my ears.

We're headed up what must surely be the only hill in Nebraska. The eighteen-wheeler we've been stuck behind since we exited 80 pulls off to the side and stops, and Chunk pulls around it.

I reach down to grab my Dr Pepper. "Sorry," I say again. Chunk just shakes his head. I debate asking another question from Truth, but conversationally speaking we are not having the best day ever.

I'm just about to click on the playlist when a giant pickup truck with blinding lights roars past us from the oncoming direction. I glimpse a shark fin on the top of the cab.

"That's the same truck from the rest stop."

"Must've left their Confederate flag back there," Chunk says.

I see the joke as a welcome sign that all is forgiven and take a drink.

The road dips and something dark shoots out across it. I stomp on an imaginary brake, Chunk hits the real brake, and we swerve. The car fills with noise, my Dr Pepper flies out of my hand, we thud against something on the side of the road, stop, and the world goes silent.

I turn my head to look at Chunk and his expression is the same as the one on my face, I'm sure. Wide eyes, slack jaw. I'm shaking.

"You okay?" are the first words out of both of our mouths. Dazed, we open our doors and get out of the car.

We're on the wide shoulder of the frontage road and Chunk walks around to my side of the car. Betty's rear panel has a long, deep scrape on it from the low stone wall she must've bumped against. There's a field beyond it and my brain is having a hard time processing anything, much less why a wall that low is there in the first place. There's a hissing sound coming from the rear passenger tire. Chunk and I just stand there looking at it.

I realize I'm still clutching the cap to the Dr Pepper and my shirt is wet with the contents of the bottle.

A dark form comes running toward us.

"Are you guys okay?"

The pieces take a second to come together but as she nears us I realize it's the girl from the rest stop with the red hair and cool boots.

Her voice wakes something up in Chunk.

"What the hell? Why would you run out in front of us like that?" he shouts, and I realize he's shaking. "We could've killed you!"

"I'm so sorry!" And when she gets closer, her eyes are wide. She is clearly as freaked out as us, but Chunk goes berserk on her.

"*We* could've been killed! You are one crazy idiot! Sane people do not run out in front of cars in the middle of the night!"

I'm freaked too, but this is a side of Chunk I've never seen.

"What the fuck?" he shouts, and the girl recoils. She doesn't come any closer.

"Look, I'm sorry," she starts to say again.

"We ALL could be dead right now!"

An image of the Incredible Hulk flashes into my mind. I touch Chunk's arm before huge green muscles can rip his sleeve to shreds.

"Easy, there, big guy," I say, and he whirls on me.

"Don't you *dare* call me *big guy*, Jer!"

Chunk doesn't say the whole thing, but hearing even part

of my old name takes me back a step. He hasn't used it in over a year.

He shakes off my hand and turns to face the girl again, pointing to the scrape on Betty and the now very flat tire.

"This tire is screwed and my car's all derpy!"

There's a pause and the girl says, "Did you say 'derpy'?" Like she can't believe her ears. "As in Derpy from *My Little Pony*?"

This stops Incredible Hulk Chunk dead. His chest deflates and he seems to come to himself.

"Just a term," he mumbles. But I could tell her that it does indeed come from *My Little Pony* and that in fact, Chunk is what we'd call a Brony, a normal guy (whatever that is) who watches *My Little Pony*.

The girl starts to say something else, and I give my head a quick shake to let her know not to pursue it. She closes her mouth and studies the car.

"But you guys are okay." She states it, like she's reminding us of what's important.

Her jacket is unzipped and her shirt is untucked.

"We're okay," I say. "Except for Betty."

"The car?" she asks, and I nod.

Chunk doesn't say anything as he walks around Betty. The only damage seems to be the flat tire and the scrape. He completes the circuit, then reopens the passenger-side door. He reaches into the glove box, takes out the rubber gloves, and grabs the owner's manual and a flashlight.

Stoic Chunk.

He flips back and forth until he finds the section he needs.

The air, so humid earlier, is cool. The girl zips up her jacket.

Headlights approach and slow. It's a truck, but not the monster truck. The passenger rolls down the window. "You need any help?"

"We're good, thanks," Chunk calls, and the truck pulls away, to my relief. We may not be all good, but we're better than we would be if a certain type stopped to help and then got a close look at me.

"Have you ever changed a tire before?" the girl asks.

"No," Chunk admits. I turn my palms up to indicate that I haven't either.

"It's easy," she says.

"I'm sure it is," Chunk says, cradling the flashlight between his ear and shoulder. "I'll just read about it right here."

"I could . . ." she starts to say.

"I've got it," he says.

She shuts up.

I walk over and hold the flashlight so Chunk can read.

I think I hear her say "Dick" under her breath. If Chunk hears it too, he doesn't react.

She watches us for a few minutes and then marches over.

"I may be a girl, but I know my way around a car. I can stand here and watch you take forever, and possibly even do it wrong so that the tire will fly off if you go above thirty miles per hour, or you can let me help."

Chunk looks up at her. "My reluctance to have your help has nothing to do with your gender. It's your lack of judgment in running out in front of the car in the first place that leads me to dismiss your ability to be helpful."

She shuts her mouth, turns on her heel, and starts walking in the direction of Ogallala.

"Hey, wait!" That thing she said about the tire flying off has me calling out to her. Still holding the flashlight, I run after her.

"Look, I'm sorry. He's really not a dick."

"Thanks, Jess!" comes a sarcastic voice from the dark behind me.

"He usually isn't. I think he's just in shock. Can you help us?"

The girl turns to face me. "I'll help *you*," she says, with the emphasis on the word *you*, leaving Chunk on his own.

"We're kind of a package deal at this point," I tell her. "But I promise to toss him out of the car once we get where we're going."

"I heard that," Chunk calls.

The girl shrugs and we walk back over to Betty.

"Your spare, and I'm hoping you have one, should be located underneath the luggage area in the back hatch."

Chunk puts down the owner's manual, stands up, and opens the back. I grab my backpack and the stick Chunk uses to prop the hood open.

A car passes us and slows down, but doesn't stop.

We get our bags out and then Chunk is digging around under the compartment. The girl and I stand looking at each other. My shirt is pretty wet. I hunch my shoulders. What can she see? And how did my voice sound?

I'm about to reach into the car and fish around for my sweatshirt when she holds out her hand. "I'm Annabelle," she says.

I shake her hand, marveling at how small it is. Does she notice how big mine is?

"Jess," I say, trying to keep my voice in a soft, in-between place. "That's Chunk." I shine the flashlight over to him.

"Chuck," he corrects. He's lit up from the cargo light inside the car. His face is a little flushed with exertion, I think. "Chuck," he repeats.

I get my sweatshirt out of the front seat. I put it on even though the sleeve is pretty soaked with Dr Pepper.

Annabelle steps toward the rear of the car.

"Your jack should be right here." She rips up the carpet mat that covers the floor of the back hatch, pulls out the jack, and carries it around to the side with the flat. She positions it underneath the car and starts to assemble what looks like a rod. I walk around to get a better look.

Chunk heaves the spare out and starts to roll it around.

"It's pretty tight here," Annabelle says, referring to the space between the low wall and the car.

He stops what he's doing.

"Wait till we get the tire off, then we can bring that one in."

There's not a lot of room to maneuver, and I end up being the one to crank the rod that lifts the side of the car. I don't mean to beat a dead horse, but have I mentioned lately that my upper body strength is waning?

Annabelle goes to work, explaining what she's doing the whole way, like it's a tutorial or something.

"You want to loosen the lug nuts in a star pattern; otherwise there's too much pressure on some and they'll be harder to get off."

One of them doesn't want to loosen anyway, and she steps up on the cross bar of the rod, putting her whole weight on it until the nut budges. I feel . . . derpy standing there holding the flashlight. Chunk stands off to the side. When I look over at him, he's staring off into space.

Annabelle is at work like a . . . a grease monkey. She gets the tire off and runs her thumb over a tear on the side.

"You're going to need a new one. They can't patch a hole in the sidewall."

She rolls it around to the rear of the car and hands it off to Chunk, exchanging it for the spare, which she calls a donut.

She hoists it into the wheel well herself, and by the time she tightens the last lug nut, I want to applaud. Even Chunk has stopped staring off into the distance. Two more cars have passed us, slowed down, but not stopped, thank God.

When Annabelle straightens up, I do applaud. So does Chunk.

"Thank you so much," Chunk says. And before she can say anything at all, he says, "Sorry I was such a dick."

She wipes her hands on her jeans. "Sorry I was such an idiot. I lost my head when I saw you guys coming over the hill. I thought I was going to get crushed against the wall."

"What were you doing out here by yourself anyway?" I ask. *Also, is Monster Truck Guy going to be out looking for you and wanting to beat up the people he finds you with?*

"Long story," she says. "Where are you headed?"

She fishes cigarettes out of her backpack.

"The Midwest," I say, just as Chunk says, "Chicago."

"You guys shouldn't drive too far with the donut. They're not supposed to be good for more than fifty miles or so."

"We're stopping in Ogallala for tonight anyway," Chunk says before I can kick him. Annabelle doesn't seem dangerous, but I've decided Monster Truck Guy is almost definitely a psychopath. Who else would drive a truck like that? Or leave his girlfriend by the side of the road and drive off?

Annabelle nods. "Tell you what. Give me a ride into Ogallala, and when the tire store opens tomorrow, I'll go with you and make sure you don't get screwed."

"Tires are tires, right? How would we get screwed?" I ask.

For the record, I'm not dead set against the plan except for the part that she could tell Monster Truck Guy where we're staying and he can kill us in our sleep.

"They're not going to want to sell you one new tire; they're going to want to sell you a set, and then balance them, and when they balance them they might find an oil leak, or a problem with the U joint." She lights a cigarette.

"And no offense, but one look at you guys with this car and your California plates and they're going to know what is so obvious to me: you don't have a clue about cars."

"How do you know so much?" Chunk asks. There's no mistaking the admiration in his voice, and I have to remind myself I can't go through life being a jealous freak about his every interaction with other girls.

"My grandma's boyfriend owned an auto shop." She takes

a drag. "And no, he never found phantom oil leaks or U joint problems when there weren't any. He's an honest guy."

She flicks ash.

"So is it a deal?"

"Deal," Chunk says.

We stand around until she's done with her cigarette.

It takes about ten minutes for us to put the jack into its compartment and then toss our luggage back into the hatch, plus the dead tire on top of that. Annabelle keeps her backpack with her.

Before she gets in the car, she whips out her phone and takes a picture of Betty's license plate and then a shot of Chunk in the driver's seat. "So the police will know who to look for if you turn out to be a psycho killer," says the girl who's been riding around middle America with a guy who drives a truck with a shark fin on top.

Betty's a two-seater, so Annabelle and I share one. It's a little tight, but not too bad, because neither of us is very big.

Up close she smells like coffee and cigarettes, and I'm aware that I smell like Dr Pepper and a locker room.

A guy's locker room.

And is it my imagination, or is she checking out my Adam's apple?

I shift away from her and a little toward Chunk.

"Why are you guys going to Chicago?"

"Jess's dad's wedding," Chunk tells her.

"Are you excited?" she asks.

"God, no!" I'm so surprised by the question and the

thought behind it that I find myself giving information I hadn't intended to. "He's marrying the cow I caught him having an affair with who used to be my mom's best friend!"

"Jess." Chunk says my name in an obnoxiously condescending tone.

"What?"

"Your parents had already split up when you found out about your dad and Jan," he says, like he's talking to a child.

"I'm sure it started before that. Yeah, they had a crappy marriage, but I'm pretty sure she's the main reason my dad left when he did!"

He shakes his head. "That's an assumption you made that might not be true."

"Still, getting together with your best friend's husband is pretty bad. No matter when it happens," Annabelle says.

I call Black Hole.

I don't want to talk about Dad or the fact that I think it's possible he and Jan were having an affair before he moved out, and that I'm pretty sure he doesn't really want me at his wedding anyway, and that I mostly came along for the road trip with Chunk, who now spends all his time texting another girl.

"What's Black Hole?" Annabelle asks.

Chunk explains it and I experience a twinge at his sharing something that's ours with her.

"So cool! I'm going to use that!"

She affects a deep voice. "Annabelle, why didn't you hand in that paper?" and then she answers in her regular voice, "Black Hole, Professor Smith. Black Hole." She laughs. "Oh man! This could revolutionize the world!" She goes into her deep voice again. "Sir, why did you run that red light?" and then, "Black Hole, officer!"

"Why did you cheat on your income taxes, Mr. Business-man?" Chunk asks. "Black Hole, IRS, Black Hole."

And I have to join in. "Why did you hack your family to bits and send them through the wood chipper? Black Hole, Judge," I say.

"Why did you bomb that defenseless country, Mr. President? Black Hole, UN. Black Hole," Annabelle says.

It goes on and on, until a smattering of lights tells us Ogallala is on the horizon.

"Where should we drop you off?" Chunk asks.

"I'm not sure," she says. "I live in Omaha. I was just headed home from school when there was a little, um, incident. Actually several incidents, which reminds me." She pulls out her phone. "I need to call my grandma."

Neither Chunk nor I say anything while she dials.

"Hey, Mamie, it's me. Sorry it's so late." I look at the clock on the dash. It's well after midnight now. "Uh-huh, everything's okay."

I'm intrigued that someone who's been dumped off by the side of the road can consider everything okay. But maybe she's just doing that thing I do, where I tell my mom I'm fine so she won't worry.

"I just wanted to let you know not to expect me tonight. I decided not to come with Landry." Chunk and I exchange glances, and I know we're thinking the same thing. *Monster truck psycho's name is* Landry?

"No, I caught a ride with a couple of other people I know from school, but we had a little car trouble. They're going to stay in a hotel tonight and I'm gonna help them out with it in the morning, then catch the bus back." She listens for a minute, then smiles. "Thanks! I was just going to ask if I could use it. Uh-huh, I'll call you when I get there. Love you!"

When she hangs up she's pretty happy.

"Well, one problem's solved. She said I could use the emergency credit card to stay in Ogallala tonight. Where are you guys heading? I'll just get a room there, too."

I hope she doesn't want to hang out when we get to the motel.

I'm still hoping for a cozy retro kitschy bad TV night, just me and Chunk.

CHAPTER 14

When we get to Ogallala we follow the GPS directions to two different motels that turn out to have no vacancies. Which is kind of weird in such a small town, but maybe there was an epidemic of cars being crashed because girls ran out in front of them and there'll be long lines at the tire stores tomorrow too.

The third motel we come to, the Husker Inn, has a vacancy sign, and we pull in under its portico. Chunk and Annabelle go to register at the front desk and I stay in the car and text my mom to tell her we're here.

MISS YOU, she texts back. Which makes me feel a little bad. Even though she was the one who encouraged me to go on this trip.

Jess: I miss you too! Should I call?
Momster: Very sweet, but I'm on my way to sleep. Let's talk tomorrow.
Jess: K

Momster: G'night. I love you more than anything.

Jess: Love you too.

I feel a twinge of guilt that I don't tell her I love her more than anything too. But it'd be weird to love your mom more than anything, right?

- - - - - -

Chunk and Annabelle come back. They're both carrying card keys and I'm relieved. It crossed my mind there might be only one room left and we'd have to share.

Chunk opens the back hatch and grabs his bag; I grab mine and the album. We walk up two flights of concrete steps and get to Annabelle's room first.

She slips the key into the door and when the light turns green, she opens it.

"You guys want to hang out?"

Before Chunk can say anything, I do a big fake yawn.

"Naw, it's late. Right?" and before he can answer, I change the subject. "What time should we get up to get the tire?"

"The shop probably opens at nine or so," she says, stepping over the threshold. Then she turns back, an uncomfortable expression on her face. "But we don't all have to go. Maybe you should stay here, Jess. Chuck and I can go."

I look at Chunk to see his reaction. I get the patented Chunk shrug.

"No, we can all go," I say. "It's okay." Is she trying to get him alone?

Annabelle bites her lower lip. "I'm not sure how to say this"—she looks up at the ceiling, like she'll find inspiration there—"and I don't want to offend you, Jess, but you might want to stay out of sight here."

Her obvious meaning stabs me and I get that immediate behind-the-eyeball ache. So much for just *being*. And Chunk lied. Clearly I'm not passing either.

I turn to head down the corridor to our room, but Annabelle grabs me. "I'm so sorry! You look great, it's just here." She touches her own neck, where her Adam's apple would be, if girls had Adam's apples, but of course they don't and I do. And now I know I wasn't being paranoid in the car. She *was* checking out my neck.

"Black Hole," I tell her. "You coming, Chunk?"

When we get into our room, I know Chunk's going to want to explore my feelings, and sure enough he opens his mouth, so I tell him Black Hole too.

I turn on the TV while he sets up his computer and turns on his Internet MicroCell.

A couple of minutes of *The Simpsons* go by, then I turn it off.

"Can you believe Monster Truck Guy's name is Landry?" I ask, to show I'm okay.

Chunk shakes his head. "Some guys have all the luck," he says.

He finishes up on the computer, gets in bed, and switches off the lamp. When I hear him start to snore, the tears finally come.

CHAPTER 15

I wake up in an unfamiliar place. It's the sensation of grit under my eyelids that reminds me where I am. I'm in Nebraska, where I should stay out of sight because I'm not passing and my eyes feel horrible because I cried myself to sleep.

Life sucks.

I have no desire whatsoever to get out of bed.

I force my eyes open, see the ugly orange-Popsicle wallpaper, and then shut them.

I roll over and open them again to look at Chunk's bed, but he's not in it. The bathroom door is ajar but the light is off.

"Chunk?" I say, just in case he decided not to be a freak like yesterday and he's actually in there without the door locked.

There's no answer, so I get up to investigate. I flip on the bathroom light and see a note on the back of the toilet.

Trust Chunk to put it in the logical place for me to find it first thing.

You were sleeping so I let you. Be back as soon as I can find a tire in this godforsaken place.

$$C$$

This blows.

I knew he was going without me but still . . . I sit down to pee, wondering how long it's going to take him. Knowing Chunk, probably a really long time. He's so deliberate about stuff. He's probably driving to every tire store in a fifty-mile radius, asking about warranties and kicking tires. Or do you only do that when you buy a car?

Oh, that's right, he went with Annabelle, who knows her way around a car. Annabelle, who made it clear I don't pass. Which is why I'm here all alone like a modern-day leper.

Is it so wrong to want to appear to the world the way I see myself?

Gray
12x17 inches
> Image: Portrait of the artist's head on a beached whale, surrounded by torn Cubs tickets, United Airlines logo, mirror shards.
> Acrylic, paper, glass, ticket stubs

Chicago hadn't gotten the message about it being spring. Dark and icy rain sleeted across the living room window of my dad and Jan's townhouse.

I shivered.

Not because it was cold inside (it wasn't) but because it was the last night of my visit, my dad was in the kitchen making me hot cocoa, and I had promised myself that I was going to tell him I was trans before I left.

The visit, my first since my dad had moved, had not been . . . a success.

Just a suck.

Freezing rain had alternated with snow since my arrival and I hadn't planned well, clothing wise. I had brought a couple of sweatshirts and jeans, and no socks to wear with my Vans. Perfect for right then in California, horrible for the arctic freeze Chicagoans call spring.

Another reason the trip sucked was that my dad had fallen back into his guy-bonding mode. Maybe he thought he'd give having a heterosexual son one last stab, because I'd undergone bowling, eating in sports-themed restaurants, and earlier that day, a Cubs game in just-above-freezing temperatures while wearing an ugly-ass parka he loaned me.

Jan was in Hawaii, visiting her sister and brother-in-law, and it felt strange being in a house she and my dad shared. Everywhere I looked there were artifacts of her. Framed prints of her photography on the walls, pillow slipcovers that I had watched her sew.

Weird too to see their books combined on the bookshelf. The Lee Child thrillers my dad liked to read, next to *History of Parisian Art of the 1920s*.

"Here you go." My dad came in and handed me a mug

before flipping on the lights. I recognized the mug as one that Jan had picked up at a student art show she and I had gone to together. The handle was shaped like a humpback whale, and I knew when I finished the cocoa I'd be able to look down and see a ceramic whale tail sticking up from the bottom.

Dad sat down at the other end of the couch and picked up the remote. I stopped him before he could click on the TV.

"I have something to tell you," I blurted, my voice louder than I'd meant it to be.

There was the briefest pause and then he put down the remote.

"I know." His voice was quiet. Resigned?

"You do?"

I knew he hadn't talked to my mom. They communicated through lawyers and me. In fact, the entire trip had been organized without them even once speaking to each other. It had been up to me to make arrangements individually with them.

"I think I've known for a while," he said, leaning toward me, making careful eye contact. "But you can't blame me for hoping I was mistaken," he said. "I'm not against gay people, it's just that life is hard enough."

"Dad, I'm not gay."

The relief on his face was palpable, and knowing what I was about to tell him would have been almost funny if I hadn't been so nervous.

"I'm trans."

"What?" He sat back against the couch suddenly and held up a hand. "Whoa, whoa, whoa!"

Like I was a horse he was trying to make stop.

My mouth soured, but I didn't sip cocoa to get rid of the taste. I knew I wouldn't be able to swallow.

He sat up again. "What makes you think that?" he demanded.

"It's just something I feel," I said, and it sounded lame even to my ears.

Too late I remembered something he used to say. *Feeling isn't the same as knowing.*

"But you don't know." His voice firm.

"What is there to know?" I don't know what I'd really expected him to say, even after role-playing this conversation with Dr. E. "I feel with my body."

"You're sixteen!" My dad jumped up and started pacing. "When I was sixteen I wanted to be a heavy metal rock star!"

Clutching my cocoa, I watched him.

"What does that have to do with anything?"

He stopped in front of the window, facing me. The light reflected off the glass and made a mirror. His shirt was untucked in back.

"People don't know their own minds when they're sixteen," he insisted.

Was he really comparing gender identity with wanting to be a rock star?

"Dad, I know my own mind and I know my own body and trust me, what's here isn't working!" I choked out the last two words and put down the mug, desperate not to cry.

He hung his head. "I shouldn't have left California."

"What? Dad, this isn't about you!"

His head came up. "Does Mary know?"

"Yes! And she's fine with it!"

He threw his hands up. "Of course she is!" he practically shouted.

"This isn't about her, Dad!" I did shout.

We stared at each other for what felt like a long time, until my dad seemed to come to some sort of resolution.

"We're going to take a little time-out here." He used his den leader voice.

He didn't hug me. He didn't cry. He just went into his bedroom and shut the door.

I sat, looking at my reflection in the window. Chin-length hair, strong jawline. I knew I was a girl, even if I didn't look like one. If I'd worn makeup and a skirt, would that have convinced him?

I sent Chunk a text: *My dad is an asshole.*

Chunk sent back a GIF of an anus with a beard.

After what felt like forever, my dad came back out and sat next to me. His hand heavy on my knee.

"Son, I know my moving was hard on you. And you might be feeling neglected, but . . ."

I scooted away from him. I didn't wait to hear what the *but* was. "You believe I'm telling you this because I want attention?"

"I think I just need to come out there more. You spend too much time alone and you think too much and it makes you question things that don't need questioning."

174

"You are so wrong!"

Dad continued in this weird soothing voice like he was a preschool teacher. My skin wanted to crawl off my body.

"I love you, but I'm sorry, Jeremy. You're male and it's a biological fact, and if you go around wearing dresses, you're just asking for trouble." His voice went from preschool to pleading. "Can't you see that?"

"You don't understand the first thing about being trans or about me!" I shouted.

"You're not trans! You're just a mixed-up kid whose parents had a rocky marriage and now you need your father in your life."

My dad looked like he was going to cry. Despite the eight million things he'd just said that were wrong, so wrong, incredibly enough, it made me sad for him.

"Dad, it's not your fault. Really," I paused. "But I am trans."

He stiffened, pulled back. "We'll agree to disagree." He stood up and went back into his room.

Left alone, I stared into my hot cocoa. I didn't see the blue whale tail until an hour later when I poured the cold, sticky brown mess into the sink.

Forget people not seeing me as female; my dad refused to even see me as trans.

— — — — — — —

I get up and make myself cardboard hotel coffee, then take a shower and shave in the bathroom. It's dim and I notice

175

that two of the three bulbs above the vanity are burned out. Fine by me.

ETA? I text Chunk when I'm done.

No idea. Crooks in this town, he texts back.

I turn on the TV and watch back-to-back episodes of *Cops*. It doesn't really distract me from the thought that I don't pass and that it was Annabelle who pointed it out. When the third episode starts my stomach growls.

Find anything yet? I text.

Nope, comes the reply. **Don't worry, Annabelle got the clerk to agree to a late checkout.**

Of course she did.

I think about Annabelle and Chunk out there, looking for tires and having a good time. Tire shopping isn't supposed to be a fun thing, but then again, Chunk and I manage to make a lot of things fun that aren't supposed to be. Or maybe it's just Chunk who's the fun one?

I make an uneventful trip to the vending machine down the hall. The peanuts are stale but I inhale them anyway when I'm back in the room. It's almost two o'clock and I'm hungry. Did it even occur to Chunk that while he went off to skip around town with Annabelle I'd be left here with no food?

STARVING, I text.

I brought the bag with the rest of the snacks in from the car. It's on the table by the window, he replies.

Okay, maybe it did occur to him.

Grabbing a handful of chips and my sketchbook, I sit down at the scuffed desk and examine yesterday's gecko with the scary clown mouth. I feel uninspired. There's nothing in this rotting budget-and-cockroach-friendly motel to inspire.

After polishing off the chips, I dig into my backpack to find my makeup kit. It's smaller than the one I use for the theater. The colors are less garish, more real. Putting makeup on myself is something I very rarely do, but I want to see that girl in the mirror again. After Annabelle's comment, I *need* to see that girl in the mirror.

It's going to suck if I can't pass next fall. For some people, passing isn't the be-all and end-all, but to me it feels like if I don't, people will view me as a freak rather than as a person just like they are.

I sit in front of the cracked mirror, painting slightly sharper brows than the ones I possess. They were thicker before I started plucking them, which is super painful, and I want to get them waxed before the end of the summer. I pull out the amazing pore-minimizing foundation that cost almost as much as I made in a full day of working at the fabric store. I line my eyes with a bronze pencil to bring out the blue, but I'm careful not to go at it with too heavy a hand. I don't want to look like a female impersonator, just a female. I like a more natural appearance except when it comes to the pièce de ré-sistance (and my favorite part). I line my lips with a deep red, and it kind of reminds me a little of Annabelle's hair. There's that girl!

I'm smiling in spite of myself when the door flies open and I hear laughing.

"Got it!" Chunk says. "Let's blow this town." He stops short when he sees me. His eyes go wide. Annabelle's right behind him. He turns around quickly. I hear him say, "See you in a few," and he shuts the door in her face.

I'm halfway to the bathroom by then.

– – – – – – –

I grab the crappy little bar soap with the edges so sharp they could cut, and smear it onto the sandpaper washcloth. Then I'm scraping at my skin. Did I just look like I was playing with makeup, *pretending* to be a girl?

"I'm sorry, Jess. I should have knocked!"

"Black Hole," I call.

How the hell do I think I'm going to show up to my dad's wedding in a dress when I freak out about what my best friend thinks when he sees me in makeup? It's not something I've ever worn around him.

I turn on the bathroom fan in order to make conversation impossible.

The girl in the mirror looked like a girl to me because I know I'm a girl, but I'm afraid it's always going to seem like I'm playing dress-up to other people, and that no one who's ever known me as Jeremy will ever really see me as a girl. Not even Chunk.

I take a long time in the bathroom, and when I get out, he's sitting at the tiny fake-wood table looking at his laptop, and he's on the phone. He looks up at me, says bye into the phone, and hangs up.

"You didn't have to take it off," he says.

"It was itchy," I say. "Let's go."

178

"Sounds like a plan." He starts unplugging and packing up. "Oh, hey,"—his voice is casual—"Annabelle needs a ride to Omaha."

The car's a two-seater, and this was supposed to be *our* road trip. A Lizzie Borden obsession is bad enough.

"I thought she was taking the bus!"

"Really, Jess?"

"What? That's what she said!"

"She really helped a lot today. And last night. It's on our way, and I think she's earned a chance not to sit on a bus for nine hours for a trip that will take four and a half by car."

"She caused the accident in the first place," I grumble.

She called me out, I want to say. *It hurt my feelings.*

Chunk sighs.

I glance at myself in the mirror.

If I'm being honest, she did it as a favor to keep me safe.

"You're right," Chunk says. "But it was an *accident*. She didn't mean it."

"Four and a half hours is all?" I ask.

"That's how far we are from Omaha."

Four and a half hours actually doesn't seem too bad, and I'll have Chunk to myself on the drive back after the wedding.

Except for when he's texting Lizzie Borden.

"Fine."

CHAPTER 16

Before we get in the car, Chunk studiously (some might say fussily) rearranges stuff in the back hatch. Annabelle grabs me.

"I feel bad about last night," she says.

"Black Hole," I tell her.

"You can't call Black Hole on an apology," she says.

Which is irritating. This time yesterday she'd never heard of Black Hole, and now she's making up new rules?

"No biggie" is what I say. "I know I don't pass," I add to show I don't care.

I mentally add the word *yet*.

"That's not true!" she exclaims. "It really was just your Adam's apple. This isn't the best place in the country to be . . . different. Still, you could have come tire shopping with us and been fine. I should have just told you to keep your chin down a little." She demonstrates, then says, "You're really pretty."

I stare at her for a minute.

Today she's wearing tan leggings and a short, flouncy skirt.

Her button-down army camouflage shirt is open to show a pink Hello Kitty tank top.

She stares back at me, and she actually looks sincere. Not like she's just trying to make me feel better.

"Oh!" she says after a second. "I brought you a donut." She pulls a little white bag from her Hello Kitty backpack. "Chuck says maple's your favorite."

By the time Chunk slams the back hatch and it's time to leave, I decide she's not *that* annoying.

Annabelle has one last smoke, and then we get into Betty. The fit is tight, but this time she's in the middle. She smells like girl shampoo.

I repeat my *no jealousy* mantra to myself and surreptitiously check out my reflection in the sideview mirror, practicing chin placement. "Did you grow up in Nebraska?" I ask as Chunk starts Betty and we pull away.

"Yup."

"But you seem so . . . tolerant."

"I think it's because my grandma was in show business. I have a whole costume parade's worth of gay 'uncles,' including one who was an actual drag queen."

"Drag queens and trans people aren't the same—" I start to say.

"I know the difference between someone who's trans and someone who cross-dresses."

Before we actually leave Ogallala, there's a little conversation about whether to detour past the UFO Water Tower, or the Sod House Museum and World's Largest Plow.

The water tower wins out, in part because we can drive

right by it on our way to the highway. Thanks to the eon it took to get a new tire, it's already well after after three o'clock. The plow and sod house would take too long since they're farther out of our way.

"We've no desiah to view any sodding houses, Guv'nuh." Chunk does an atrocious English accent.

We drive slowly past the tower, which is just a tower with the top round part painted to look like a UFO. Little aliens peek out of porthole windows. Apparently at night it lights up.

I check it off the list, confident that it is an infinitely better investment of time than the plow would have been.

When we get on I-80, Annabelle notices the dash cam. "What's this?" she asks, touching it.

"Nothing," Chunk says quickly.

I can't believe it. Is Chunk trying to pretend we are less nerdy than we are for Annabelle's benefit?

"His idea," I say, reaching over and flicking it on. "Captain's Log, Stardate 11706.16. First mate reporting we've picked up a Klingon."

Annabelle laughs. "Are you guys Trekkies?"

"No," Chunk says.

"Not really," I say. "But someone seems awfully interested in visiting the Future Birthplace of Captain James T. Kirk."

"Oh! In Riverside! Landry went once. I think there's supposed to be a big festival this week."

"Really? Chunk, did you know about this?" I ask.

"Landry the Monster Truck Guy?" Chunk asks.

"The one and only," Annabelle confirms. "He loves *Star Trek*."

"And leaving girls by the side of the road," I say.

"Just me," she says. "And actually, he didn't leave me. I got out and wouldn't get back in. He drove off, and then an hour and a half later got worried about me. He texted and called easily thirty times between last night and this morning. I told him to fuck off every single time. He finally stopped when I said I was going to use my phone log as proof of harassment if he didn't knock it off."

"He knew he left you all alone in the middle of nowhere and he waited almost two hours before getting worried?" I ask.

"I can take care of myself." Annabelle reaches down into her (fabulous) boots and pulls pepper spray out of one, and a slim knife out of the other.

"Holy shit! You're a badass!" I exclaim.

The handle and blade are one piece, but the blade has to be five inches of very sharp-looking steel.

"You've never stabbed anyone, though, right?"

"Never had to, but you should get one and learn how to use it, Jess. A girl's gotta be prepared to protect herself."

My insides flush pleasantly warm when she says that. It feels like . . . sisterhood or something.

"Dude, isn't a knife with a blade that long illegal?" Chunk asks, eyeing it sideways.

"You know? I've never asked," she says, slipping her self-defense tools back into her footwear.

"Even with a knife, getting out of a truck in the middle of the night in the middle of nowhere still doesn't seem like a great idea," Chunk says, like he's someone's dad.

Annabelle rolls her eyes for the second time in two minutes. "I realize that. What are you, some kind of a valedictorian?"

He smirks, and then asks, "Why did you do it?"

Annabelle exhales loudly. It's a sound somewhere between a sigh and a growl.

"He asked me to marry him."

"That seems like a reasonable response to a proposal," I say, just as Chunk exclaims, "Marry him? How old are you?"

"I could do that thing where I make you guess, but that'd be pretty annoying. I'm almost twenty. But I was seventeen when I graduated from high school.

"It wasn't just the proposal that made me break it off for good; it's that he cheated on me constantly and thought he could get away with it." Her tone is matter-of-fact and the set of her mouth seems more exasperated than wounded, somehow.

"I once overheard him tell a buddy that it's just a biological fact that guys need more sex than girls, which means that in the natural order men are *supposed* to cheat." She rolls her eyes.

"So for almost four years you've been hanging out with a guy who you knew cheated on you?" Chunk asks. "I've *got* to change up my game."

I want to ask him *what* game.

Instead I ask Annabelle why she was with him in the first place.

She does that sigh-growl thing again.

"We got together when I was a junior in high school. He was a senior, and I know it sounds shallow . . . well, it is shallow, but what attracted me to him at first was that he was good-looking and popular. And he seemed smart."

"Smart?" I can't believe a smart person would drive a vehicle like his, but that's just me.

"I'm smart in school, but he was smart in a different way," Annabelle says.

"So you guys were that golden couple," I say.

"Nope."

"You weren't?" I'm surprised.

Again, her tone is matter-of-fact. "He was popular, but I was a nerd."

"Nerds rule the world," Chunk says, no doubt picturing himself sitting on a throne and wearing a crown.

"Yeah, that news hasn't really reached the high schools in Nebraska yet." Annabelle smiles. "Anyway, Landry has a gift for making a gal feel incredibly special, which is pretty amazing when you've been accustomed to people looking past you, or worse, noticing you and calling you four-eyes."

I don't know if I believe her. It's hard for me to reconcile her attention-getting hair and clothes with the image of a nerd.

"I'd get sweet texts, random phone calls just to say he was thinking of me. Stuff like that. The strange thing is, once I quit hiding in the shadows and having a little confidence in myself, he started cheating on me."

She stares out the windshield for a minute and there's just the sound of the road under Betty's tires.

"I was devastated the first couple of times I caught him, but he apologized and blamed it on being drunk, and in one case on the fact I'd gone to visit relatives and he missed me."

"What an asshole!" Chunk bursts out.

"I know, I know! And it's pathetic, but I took him back. And then when I left for college, he followed me. I thought that showed his devotion, and that meant he'd be faithful, but it turned out there was just a wider pool of girls for him there." Growl-sigh.

"For the last year or so we've been more cat and mouse than boyfriend and girlfriend. Every time I suspected him of cheating I'd go on the hunt, searching through his phone and hacking into his e-mail to catch him—and I started to get a weird exhilaration when I did—because he thought he was so smart, but busting him proved I was the smart one. Pretty sick, huh?"

"I don't know about sick, but I'd say exhausting," Chunk tells her.

"It was that, too," Annabelle admits. "Anyway, the final straw came last night when I recited word for word a private message he'd sent to some girl named Bethany, as proof I knew he'd been with her, and he told me that we should get married, and then he'd respect the vows."

"No way!" Chunk is really into the story. *No jealousy!*

"Something clicked. Seriously, I knew I wasn't in love with him. What I was in love with was the crazy adrenaline rush I got from catching him in his lies. Once I pictured spending the rest of my life playing detective, I knew we were done."

"But you got out of the truck in the middle of nowhere! Couldn't you have waited to get to civilization?" Chunk asks.

"What can I say? I was too busy savoring the last *whoosh-zap* of biochemicals in my brain to care where I was."

"Maybe you should take up skydiving," Chunk says.

"Or bungee jumping," I say.

"I'll bet bungee jumping from the wing of an airplane would stimulate you sufficiently," Chunk tells her.

"Thanks for the suggestions. I'll be sure to ignore them." Annabelle leans back into the seat. There's a half smile on her face, and she really does look content. "Anyway, it's all over with Landry for real now. My grandma'll be happy. She never liked him."

"What about your parents?" I ask. It's getting easier to be nosy.

"They died in an accident when I was four."

And the mood in the car, so silly a minute ago, becomes quiet, and stays that way for a while.

I stare off into green fields of corn, thinking about what it would feel like to have dead parents. I remember telling Chunk my dad was dead to me after he refused to sign the waiver.

Obviously, even if I had kept my vow never to talk to my dad again (clearly I'm a vow-breaker here, or getting ready to be one), it wouldn't have been the same as if he were deceased.

As long as he was alive, there'd at least be the possibility that someday he'd remember the last conversation we ever had, and regret it.

Lavender

8x8 inches

Portrait of the artist posed after Munch's *The Scream*.
Acrylic on canvas

I chewed the inside of my cheek while I waited for my dad
to pick up his phone. It was March in my junior year and it
had been just over ten months since my miserable trip to
Chicago. I'd seen my dad twice since then. Once over the
summer when he'd taken me camping in Tahoe, and at
Christmastime, when he'd come out to take me to Disney-
land. He didn't bring up Jan either time.

Neither visit was easy. Gender identity was something I
was talking about every Monday with Dr. E, and thinking
about constantly, but there were lots of awkward silences
with my dad while we both avoided the subject.

Now it was almost spring (the real kind, not the Chicago kind) and I was done waiting for my dad to respond to
the e-mail I'd sent.

Dear Dad,

I know this is a hard thing for us to talk about, but
I'm hoping that writing you about it will be easier.

I've had a long time to think and to talk to Dr. E,
and here is what I need to do.

Next fall I'll be applying to the art schools I told
you about, and I want to enroll at whichever accepts
me (fingers crossed for RISD or Stern) as Jessica
Saunders.

When I show up, I DON'T WANT TO BE "THAT TRANSGENDER KID."

I want everyone to see me as I see myself. As a girl.

In order to make that transition, I need to start taking hormones so that my outsides will match the way I feel inside. The idea is that I would start with the lowest possible dose, and the physical changes would be very gradual over my senior year. Not noticeable unless you were really looking for them, in order to avoid being hassled, or having to answer a lot of questions from the kids at school. (This also takes care of your concern that people might want to attack me for being trans.) The summer after graduation, I'd be able to up the dose if my body will tolerate it.

I know it's hard for you to understand that I'm really female, but I'm hoping you'll at least consider this, because it is VITAL to my HEALTH AND WELL-BEING.

The thing is, since you and mom share custody, and I won't be 18 until next November, I need both your signatures in order to get the hormones.

Please, please, please think about this.

Dr. E and Dr. Hue both say they would be happy to have a telephone appointment with you to discuss concerns you might have.

Please, please, please. The only thing that keeps me going is the thought that it won't always be this way, that I won't always be this way.

If you want to answer in an e-mail that's okay, or you could call when you get this.

Jess

Two torturous days had gone by and I hadn't heard back.

Chunk tried to tell me that maybe this meant my dad was considering it. I hoped he was right, but really, radio silence for two days couldn't mean anything good.

When I couldn't stand it anymore, I dialed his number.

He picked up on the sixth ring.

"Jeremy?"

Thank God. I hate leaving messages, and who knows what I would have said.

"Did you get my e-mail?" I asked, not bothering to say hello.

Silence. I stared up at the poster over my bed.

"Dad?"

It sounded like he cleared his throat.

"I did," he said, slowly.

"So I can send you the form, or maybe scan it and you can send it back."

"Jeremy, I think this is something we need to talk about in person."

"I don't see why."

I listened to him breathe for a moment before he spoke again.

"It's complicated, and I'd like us to be together in the same room when we have this conversation."

I knew what that meant.

"So you're not going to sign."

"Jeremy, I really don't want us to talk about this over the phone."

"So you can tell me in person that you don't care about my well-being?"

"We both know that's not true!" My dad's voice jumped half an octave. "This is coming out of the blue! I'd be a piss-poor father if I let you do something like this to yourself because you were going through a phase!"

"This is not coming from out of the blue!" I was momentarily incapable of articulating much more than this; there was a gaping hole in my stomach.

As much as his refusal had been expected on some level, I realized I'd really held a shred of hope that he would say yes.

"It's not a phase, Dad!"

"Honey, I'm sorry."

I didn't hear sorry in the way he said it.

"Won't you at least talk to Dr. E?" I hated the groveling sound of my own voice.

"That's not going to help anything. Look, why don't we shelve this conversation until we see each other when you come out to visit this summer?"

Incredible!

"Dad." My voice shook. "Here's something you have to know. This is the most important thing in my life. If you don't agree to sign for the hormones, I won't be coming to visit you. Ever." I meant it with every muscle fiber in my body, every cell.

I closed my eyes.

There was a silence on the other end of the phone, before my dad said, "I'm sorry you feel that way right now."

I hung up on him.

I lay on my bed for a long time, feeling something like hatred. I stared at the poster above my bed: Edvard Munch's *The Scream.*

Surely the subject of the painting just had their whole gender identity dismissed as a phase.

My dad called me back.

I blocked his number.

I never opened his e-mails.

Physical mail arrived, and I stored it unopened in my closet.

CHAPTER 17

We pass a sign for the Fort Cody Trading Post.

"Oh my God, we *have* to stop," Annabelle says.

I open the glove compartment and take out Chunk's roadside attraction printout. "It's not on the list," I say.

"Then someone didn't do their research!" Annabelle says. "This is the best place in Nebraska!"

So we stop. Annabelle lights a cigarette as soon as we get out of the car.

For the record, the best place in Nebraska, according to someone born and raised there, is a gigantic tourist trap and gift shop.

Maybe the biggest one ever.

And it truly is remarkable. In the parking lot we're greeted by a gigantic two-dimensional Buffalo Bill, visible for miles around, I'm sure. It's the kitsch I've been looking for since we left California. We take several pictures. I'm careful to keep my chin down.

"He totally could have kicked Godzilla's ass," I marvel.

"Provided he mistook Godzilla for a buffalo," Chunk says.

"It certainly is impressive," I tell Annabelle.

"Just wait," she says, puffing away.

"Did Bill Cody establish this before or after he massacred all the buffalo in America and deprived the Native Americans of what, up until then, had been a sustainable source of food?" Chunk asks.

Annabelle ignores his comment but tosses her smoke to the ground, grabs his hand, and starts dragging him to the fort.

He seems only too willing to go along.

I step on her cigarette to put it out and follow them, chanting *no jealousy, no jealousy, no jealousy* in my head.

The nicotine-addicted girl with the knife and pepper spray in her boots can't wait to show us the dummies manning the stockade towers, especially the one with the arrow sticking out of his butt.

When we get to the entrance, Annabelle lets go of Chunk's hand.

And I remind myself that really the fun of a place like this is in just going with it.

We are treated to a diorama of Buffalo Bill's Wild West Show that includes twenty thousand hand-carved figures, Annabelle tells us proudly, as if she'd made them herself.

A recorded voice comes on, and miniature horses start moving along a track on the perimeter. Little bulls buck, cowboys ride and rope. We watch the whole thing, wandering around the display to see everything.

I am aware that it's getting later, and we're still a few hours from Omaha, so we should get back on the road quickly, but I'm drawn in by the painstaking detail in the folk art.

Annabelle's transfixed by the tableau of a crowd watching a trapeze show.

"I love this place," she says. "When I was a kid, my uncle would take me on road trips and we always stopped by here. I use to dream of magically turning small so I could run around with all the little people and swing on the swings."

"Did you get out of the car and refuse to get back in?" I tease. She hip-checks me.

When the show's over, we wander the rest of the place with its artifacts of old saddles and cowboy boots. I'm ready to leave before Annabelle and Chunk are. I can't tell if Chunk is really interested in looking at rawhide whips or if he's just being polite.

"I'm going to buy some candy and then I'll meet you outside," I say, and Annabelle snaps to attention.

"Wait a second! I've been saving the best for last!" And she leads us over to a (taxidermied) two-headed calf.

We stare at it in mute wonder.

"America," Chunk finally says, doffing an imaginary hat and placing it over his heart.

We spend another longish time after that browsing through an impressive array of souvenirs. Whoopee cushions, steer heads, baby bibs, Nebraska-made food, and tons of cowboy and Native American detritus.

In the end, I buy some homemade fudge. Chunk buys a little plastic buffalo to stick to Betty's dashboard, and Annabelle buys a few surprisingly nice little silver hairclips. Some with turquoise, some inlaid with black and white beads, and, for the kitsch factor, one with a pair of tiny moccasins stuck to it.

Chunk goes to the bathroom and we head out to the car.

"This could take a while," I tell Annabelle.

I've had the spare key since just after getting locked out at Mel's in Wyoming, but we don't get in. Instead, we both sit on Betty's hood.

Across from us, a van with handicapped license plates has just parked. An old man gets out and walks over to the sliding door on the passenger side. The door opens and an elevator thing comes out with a little old lady in a wheelchair on it. It lowers her to the ground, and when she gets there the old man brushes a kiss across the top of her head. Seeing them gives me a pang.

"I'll bet they've been together since they were kids," I say. "I kind of wonder if being married to someone who's known you forever would make life more complicated."

Annabelle nods. "Like they've known you for longer so they'll remember more of the stupid stuff you've said and done."

"Exactly!" I say, and we smile at each other.

"I really like the way you dress, by the way," I tell her.

Annabelle grins. "Thanks! Chunk says you're a really good artist, so that means a lot to me."

"Nah, it shouldn't." I smile at her. "Artists aren't necessarily known for their fashion sense. Just look at me." I gesture to my plain blue T-shirt and skinny jeans to indicate that my personal style is no style. "I wouldn't have thought to pair Hello Kitty with camo, or camo with a skirt for that matter."

"A year or two ago I figured out I should dress to please myself," Annabelle says. "I'm happy if someone likes what I'm wearing but I literally couldn't give a rat's ass if they don't."

"Which is a good thing," I tell her, "because rat's asses are probably messy to get, and to *literally* give them to people who don't like the way you dress would be a lot of trouble."

She sticks out her tongue, but then looks thoughtful.

"I know you guys have a schedule to keep. What time's the wedding tomorrow?"

"Six," I say, and my old friend anxiety slides into the drop-in center that is my gut. I truly do not know if my dad even really wanted me there when he invited me, and I still have no idea what I'm going to say to him.

You'd think that as someone who had a front-row seat to the knock-down, drag-out that was my parents' marriage I'd be better at confrontation myself.

"P.m., of course," Annabelle says.

I nod. I have a whole twenty-five hours to figure out what the hell I'm doing.

"And what are you going to wear?"

"I don't know," I lie, thinking of the Muzzy dress. I don't want her to ask me to model it for her.

"I don't believe you," she says, but not in a mean way. "I'll bet you've had your outfit picked out since you decided to go. But that's okay." She leans back and appraises me. "We're about the same size, aren't we?"

I nod, glad that even though my dad didn't have the decency to sign a waiver for the hormones, at least he did pass down to me his diminutive genes. He's only five foot eight, and I'm even shorter than that.

"Something I do with my other girlfriends is trade clothes around. We all wear it differently, but I have a bunch of cute stuff that'd look good on you. When you guys drop me off I could let you see if there's anything you want. Interested?"

I nod, fighting the urge to ask why she's being so nice to me . . . does it matter that she's feeling sorry for me if I get cool clothes like hers?

"Oh . . . and one thing I think you should do . . ." Reaching forward, she rakes my hair with her fingers, parting it off-center. It feels weird. Before I can shake it back into its natural middle part, she whips open the bag from the gift shop and puts a clip in the side that now has more hair.

Annabelle leans back to study the effect and smiles. She digs a compact out of her backpack and opens it so I can see myself in the mirror, and when I do, the harp in my heart thrums. With my hair swept to the side just above my brows, my gigantic forehead is gone! Or at least camouflaged.

I reach up to touch the clip with my right hand. It's the silver black-and-white beaded one. It would go perfectly with the Muzzy dress.

"I've got to get some of these."

Annabelle hands me the bag.

"Is this just because you feel sorry for calling me out?"

I sound ungracious.

"Don't be stupid. It's because you were nice to me when Chuck wasn't, after I almost got you killed. It's because you let me horn in on a trip that's supposed to be your adventure with your best friend."

And now I feel bad for giving Chunk a hard time about taking her to Omaha.

She goes on. "It's because you came with me to one of my favorite places in the world, and yeah, it's tacky, but you didn't make me feel bad about liking it."

I nod.

"And okay, maybe I do feel a little bad about last night, because I think I gave you the impression that you stick out more than you do. I'm just paranoid about the world."

"Why are *you* paranoid?"

She takes a cigarette out of her backpack and lights it before answering.

"Remember my uncle the drag queen?"

I nod. I think I know what's coming, and it makes me queasy.

"He was jumped one night and beaten by a group of guys who were going to 'teach the faggot a lesson.' He's in assisted care with a traumatic brain injury. Fifty years old and has to use a walker."

It makes me want to get in the car and lock the doors.

"Here in Nebraska?"

She takes a drag and shakes her head. "That might be the worst part of it." She exhales. "New York City."

And she's right. That does seem even worse somehow. Like there's not a truly safe place anywhere.

– – – – – – –

When Chunk comes back, we slide down off Betty's hood.

Annabelle smooths my hair next to the clip. "What do you think?" she asks Chunk.

He tilts his head sideways and looks. The tips of my ears feel warm.

"Nice" is all he says in an offhand voice. He opens the door and gets in.

I stoop to the sideview mirror and have another look at my forehead-minimizing hairstyle. I don't care what he says. It's better than nice.

CHAPTER 18

An hour later, we're playing Trivial Pursuit. Annabelle and Chunk are engaged in a death battle.

When she gets the answer to "What is the driest place on Earth?" (the Atacama Desert in Chile) Chunk's admiration is anything but grudging.

I repeat my mantra to myself.

No jealousy, no jealousy, no jealousy.

And I spend a lot of time stealing surreptitious glances of my new hairstyle in the sideview mirror and ignoring the *whoosh*es of incoming texts on Chunk's phone.

"Where are you guys planning to stop tonight?" she asks.

"Riverside, Iowa," Chunk says.

"But the wedding's not until six o'clock tomorrow?"

She takes out her phone and does some calculation. "It's only a few hours to Chicago from there." She shifts a little in the seat. "I have some clothes I want to get rid of and Jess could try some on, and I want you guys to meet Mamie and Joe."

Chunk doesn't say anything.

"I think you should spend the night at my house and then just get an early start in the morning."

"We couldn't do that," Chunk says.

"Why not? There's plenty of room, and Mamie loves company."

"We need to get to Riverside," Chunk says.

"I don't get why we have to go there tonight," I say. New clothes sound better to me than the Future Birthplace of Captain Kirk. "Why can't we stop on the way back and then loop down to 40?"

"If you guys got an early enough start, you could stop in Riverside and still get to the wedding in plenty of time."

"Sounds like a plan," I say firmly.

Cool girl clothes, free! Wheeee!

- - - - - - -

We stop at a Hardee's just before Omaha. Both Annabelle and I have a Thickburger El Diablo with bacon and chipotle sauce. Chunk gets a low-carb little Thickburger.

It's getting dark by the time we get to the turnoff for Annabelle's.

After the turnoff, there's a narrow road lined with cornstalks. Annabelle directs Chunk onto another road, and finally we leave the pavement and hit gravel. A white fence hugs the road we're on now, and we drive through a gate.

As we do, Annabelle says, "Oh. I told Mamie I know you

guys from the University of Wyoming. Also, something I forgot to tell you. Mamie hasn't left the house since before I was born. She's agoraphobic."

Delayed information much?

Gravel crunches under Betty's wheels. There's something a little picture-postcardish about the way the headlights shine on the front of the old farmhouse.

Chunk stops the car and two huge dogs run up to Betty, barking. When Annabelle gets out, they nearly knock her over. It's not that I'm afraid of dogs exactly, but I don't like when they jump up on me and rip my throat out.

Man, I hate when they do that.

"Easy! Easy!" Annabelle is saying, but she's patting them. The dogs nuzzle her and lick her and when one starts to lose interest and comes over to sniff the car, I shut the door before it can get to me.

Annabelle's tone changes. "Sit!" she commands, and they both do.

"She's like a Bene Gesserit witch from *Dune*," I say to Chunk, who also seems nervous to leave the car. "That *voice*."

"It's okay to get out now. They're just excited," she calls. "They really won't hurt you."

I make no move to get out of the car.

"C'mon, you guys."

"I'll go first," Chunk says, throwing open his door.

I get out slowly. Annabelle is headed up the walk already. We follow her and the dogs follow us, sniffing.

A yellow porch light shines from above the front door.

"So you don't like dogs?" Annabelle says.

"I love them," I say.

"Jess is lying," Chunk says.

"I can tell," Annabelle says. "But these two are sweet. They won't hurt you unless you try and raid the henhouse."

Hearing the term "raid the henhouse" coming out of Annabelle's mouth is a little odd, what with her asymmetrical fire-alarm red hair and hipster glasses.

The front door is open with just the screen door closed, and as we get closer, we can hear the sound of a television turned to what sounds like a game show. In Spanish. I catch a whiff of Pine-Sol.

We step inside and Annabelle hollers, "Mamie? Joe? We're here. Tell the dancing boys to hide!

"Family joke," she says. She leads us down a hallway that opens onto a large, old-fashioned living room with walnut paneling that goes halfway up the walls, then stops where flocked red-and-gold wallpaper takes over. The room looks like something out of a museum, and it doesn't seem very farmy to me.

"Mamie, here are the friends I told you about," Annabelle says, and I try not to react because she's saying it to one of the biggest human beings I have ever seen in the flesh. Really.

Mamie looks like a mound of clay molded to the sofa, roughly the shape and nearly the size of a mud hut. Okay, that may be an exaggeration, but she is huge—four hundred pounds, I'll bet.

I'm staring at her with what I'm sure must be the idiot look of shock on my face when I become aware that there is also a normal-sized human next to her on the couch. I realize he sees me staring and the expression on his face is not so friendly. I look over at Chunk to see his reaction.

His eyes don't meet mine.

Annabelle crosses the braided rug and stoops to kiss Mamie. She also kisses the man, interrupting his unfriendly glare, and then he smiles and looks pleased.

The dogs run over to the couch.

"This is my friend Jess from school," Annabelle says, then adds, "and her friend, Chuck. This is my grandma, Margaret Nelson."

"Call me Mamie," the gigantic lump on the couch instructs.

Chunk crosses the braided rug to lean down and shake Mamie's hand.

"Oh, and this is Joe," Annabelle says.

We get through all of the how-do-you-dos. Mamie invites us to sit anywhere.

I take a seat on the piano bench.

"Annabelle, be a sweetie and get us a beer," Mamie says. "You'll have one too, right?" she asks Chunk and me. "I know you college kids like your beer."

Joe chuckles soundlessly.

Chunk and I exchange glances. We're not really drinkers.

Mamie says, "And get crackers and some of the cheese that's in the crock."

"I will, but you have to turn off the TV and talk to my friends while I'm in the kitchen," Annabelle bosses.

"Where are my manners? Of course," Mamie says, fishing for the remote from under a bowl that's next to her on the couch, upsetting it. Popcorn spills all over the floor and the dogs go wild eating it up. It's mayhem a-go-go. When it's over, there isn't a kernel left anywhere, but the TV's off.

"What were you watching?" I ask.

"*Sábado Gigante*," Mamie says. "It's a Mexican game show."

"She doesn't speak Spanish," Annabelle calls from the kitchen. "She just has a thing for Latinos. And for Joe, even though he's not."

Joe, evidently a man of few words, smiles.

"Tell me about your studies," Mamie says loudly, looking toward the kitchen.

Before Chunk and I can make up answers, she leans forward and whispers, "And please tell me she's rid of that Landry for good!"

Chunk and I eye her nervously. The squirrels in my brain are holding up a sign that says DON'T GET INVOLVED.

"It certainly seems as though that might be over," Chunk says.

I look at him and he lifts one shoulder.

Joe speaks up for the first time. "Nothing against the boy. We just don't want her to give up her studies."

"And I don't like him!" Mamie hisses.

"I know you're gossiping, because you're whispering!"

Annabelle calls from the kitchen. There's the sound of cabinets opening and shutting.

"Just asking Chuck and Jess about their studies," Mamie calls.

"Bullshit," Annabelle trills. She sounds like a Disney princess.

"Computer science," Chunk says loudly.

"Art," I say.

"Oh! I thought at least one of you would have been in premed, like Annabelle!"

Premed? This smoking girl with black fingernail polish and crazy magenta hair is studying to be a doctor? The hair must have come after her college interview.

"Stop gossiping!" Annabelle calls.

"Stop smoking!" Mamie calls back.

Annabelle walks into the room carrying a tray. Chunk jumps up to help her.

"Thanks," she says to him. She sticks her tongue out at Mamie. "Grrrr," she says, placing the tray on a little table next to the couch. She pours beer into glasses that are shaped like cowboy boots and passes around a plate of cheese and crackers.

"None for you," Mamie says to the dogs, who are lying on the floor next to the couch. Popcorned out, I guess. One of them gives a halfhearted thump of his tail.

I eat a cracker and sip from my cowboy boot. The beer is cold but bitter. I'm thirsty, so I take a few swigs.

"Where did you all say you were headed?" Mamie asks.

"Chicago," I say.

"Oh! I love Chicago," Mamie exclaims. "We used to go there all the time." She takes a dainty sip of beer. I notice mine is half empty already.

"Mamie doesn't go anywhere anymore," Annabelle says. I glance over at Mamie to see how she takes this. Was it a dig?

"It's true, I don't get out in the world anymore, but Annabelle brings the world to me," Mamie says cheerfully, taking a sip of her beer.

To keep myself from gulping down the rest of mine, I set my glass down on an end table and stand up to look at the photos on the wall. There's one that catches my eye, and I step closer to get a better look.

"Why Chicago?" Mamie asks.

"Jess's dad is getting married," Annabelle answers.

In the picture, a beautiful woman stands onstage before footlamps, roses in her arms. Her hair is swept over one shoulder, and she wears a dreamy look on her face.

"This is really lovely," I say, turning to the rest of the room.

"Do you know who that is?" Mamie asks. And I rack my brain for the names of opera stars from years gone by. I look to Chunk helplessly.

"Maria Callas?" he asks. Rescuing me.

Mamie's eyes light up. "How kind of you to say so! No, that's me!"

"Mamie's an opera singer," Annabelle says.

"Was," Mamie corrects.

"Is," Annabelle insists, scooting onto the piano bench. She

quickly shuffles through the sheet music, and pulls out something called *Ruhe Sanft* (I only know the name because I looked over her shoulder).

"Don't do it," Mamie warns.

Annabelle just grins and starts to play. Notes trill and flutter through the air and I'm absorbing yet another side of this cigarette-smoking, camo-wearing, Hello Kitty–obsessed premed student: she is also an amazing pianist. Then a mind-blowing, ethereal sound fills the air. I turn and look over at Mamie, who has not shifted from her position on the couch. Her mouth is open, her eyes are closed, and it's clear she can't help herself. She's singing because she can't not sing. Impossible notes come from somewhere inside her.

I don't know a lot about music, but I do know there's a reason people stand to sing. It has to do with breath support and body mechanics. There is no way she should be able to produce this magic from that position. But she does.

And an even more amazing thing happens. I can see her, not as she is now, but as she was then. I see the Mamie of the picture. I find in her doughy cheeks the outline of the strong jaw and fine planes of her face, and I want to sketch her more than I've wanted to sketch anything in my life. I want to capture the magnificence that is Mamie.

"That's enough for now," Mamie says. There's a bead of sweat running down her face. Joe tenderly reaches over with a handkerchief to dab at it and she closes her eyes again and smiles.

"That was all a long time ago," she says.

One of the dogs thumps its tail in sympathy.

"Amazing," I say as I finish my beer. "Thank you so much."

Mamie opens her eyes again and looks at me.

"Thank you for listening to an old lady."

- - - - - - -

Annabelle gets us more beer, and Chunk does his debonair-with-the-old-ladies Chunk thing. He asks all the right questions. Where she's performed (Europe and the major cities in the US), her favorite opera (Verdi's *Falstaff*, a great comedy as well). He even gets her to talk about the reason she hasn't left the house in twenty years (panic attacks).

We settle back, drinking and talking. Mamie tells stories of touring in Europe, and Joe smiles and doesn't say much. Annabelle puts on some old music.

"I love Glenn Miller," Mamie says. "I once met him when we were both in Philadelphia . . ." And she's off telling another story. Every once in a while, I look up to find Joe's eyes on me. Annabelle refills my beer again and I don't mind the taste at all. Things are getting a little fuzzy around the edges.

Eventually conversation winds down, and Mamie's closing her eyes for longer and longer moments. I'm not feeling so spritely myself.

Mamie dozes off eventually, and Annabelle puts her finger to her lips and starts gathering up plates and glasses. Chunk and I stand to help her. They head into the kitchen and I'm following, but I pause at Mamie's photograph again, a little hazy. I'm trying to memorize the lines so I can sketch her from memory. Mamie is snoring softly now, and the dogs have been let out. Joe stands next to me, looking at the photo too.

"People are always more than one thing," he says.

CHAPTER 19

"Let me show you where you guys are going to sleep," Annabelle says, after putting the dishes into the sink. The kitchen is old-timey and looks more like what my idea of a farmhouse should look like. The wooden cabinets are red, and the wallpaper has roosters on it. "Then you can come talk to me while I smoke," she says.

"I'm with Mamie. You're a med student. How can you do that to yourself?" I ask.

"Premed," she says. "And you'd be surprised at how many of us do."

She leads us through the doorway and up a narrow flight of stairs to a room with twin beds. Between them is an open window, and a hint of a breeze comes through.

"This used to be my room, until I convinced Mamie to let me move into the one off the porch. Easier to sneak out for a smoke there," she explains. "Speaking of which, let's go."

I shake my head. "I'm not contributing to your delinquency," I say.

The truth is, despite my wooziness, I want to get out my sketchbook while the Mamie face transformation is fresh in my mind. Dimly it occurs to me that I want to do a piece on her, and that for the first time in a long time, the finished work won't have a self-portrait in it. This one will be all about Mamie.

"Whatever," Annabelle says. "C'mon, Chuck." And he follows her.

"Don't do anything I wouldn't do," I say, sitting on the bed. Two sets of eyes roll in unison.

I throw my backpack onto the bed closest to the window, sit down next to it, and pull out my sketchpad. I grab my vine charcoal, and go to work. It feels unwieldy at first, like my fingers are too thick, and somewhere it occurs to me that my coordination isn't quite spot-on because maybe I am a little tipsy. I keep drawing, though, trying to capture what I thought I saw. Mamie's young self through the lens of her older, bigger self.

Somewhere below, a screen door creaks open and snaps shut.

"Thanks for hanging with me and letting me indulge my vice," Annabelle says. They are standing directly underneath the window.

"Thanks for giving us a place to stay," Chunk says. There's the sound of a lighter clicking. Something about the acoustics makes it sound as though it's all happening right next to my head.

"So how long have you guys known each other?" Annabelle asks.

"Forever," Chunk says. "We were in first grade together."

The smell of smoke wafts in through the window.

I pause in my sketching. I don't remember that far back, but Chunk is the smart one, so if he says it, it must be so.

"Can I ask a nosy question?" Annabelle asks. I giggle inside a little at that, because she asks nosy questions all the time, as far as I can tell.

"Fire away," Chunk says.

"When did she start transitioning?"

"Pretty recently, but it's been a long time coming," Chunk says.

"Is it weird for you? After always having known her as a guy?" Annabelle asks.

A pilot light ignites in my stomach.

What if I don't like what he says?

"It's fine," Chunk says, and I'm relieved. My charcoal smooths the line of Mamie's jaw.

"She's just Jess. Doing her own thing. My mom and I always knew she was gay, and when she came out as trans, it all made even more sense to us."

Mamie's jaw gets suddenly thick because I'm pushing down too hard. Made more sense to *us*? *Chunk* did *tell his mom!*

"You're a good friend to her," Annabelle says, and there's a fire in my gut. I want to charge down the stairs and point out the flawed logic in this compliment. Good friends do *not* reveal secrets they've been charged with keeping.

"It can be challenging. Jess is pretty much all about

herself right now. My mom says that's normal and that it'll change, but sometimes I worry a little it won't."

WTF?

"Okay. Another nosy question. Now that you know she's a girl, could you see yourself liking her like that?"

Any thought of running downstairs and pounding Chunk for telling his mom and for talking shit about me to Annabelle halts. I sit straight up, flames licking my heart.

"It has nothing to do with whether she's a girl or not; I'm pan. It's that she's my best friend."

"Pan as in the guy with goat feet?" Annabelle's laughing, but not in a mean way.

"No. You know. Pansexual. Attracted to any individual based on something other than their secondary characteristics."

I suck in my breath. He's never said anything about this to me, and yet here he is confiding in someone he just met?

You never ask me. We're always talking about your feelings. What you like, what you don't like. When was the last time you asked me anything about me?

"Plus I have a girlfriend. Well, kind of. I'm supposed to meet up with a girl in Riverside."

And all the shitty pieces fall into place. Captain's Log, Stardate. His sudden stupid effing interest in *Star Trek*.

Betrayal doesn't even begin to cover it. I want to scream and throw a tantrum the way my mom used to.

When exactly was he going to tell me? Not that it matters. I look down at my sketchbook. Mamie's face has only partially taken shape; there's the outline of her rounded cheeks and the hammock of her jaw, but she's not there yet. I'm smashing vine charcoal between my fingers, making a mess, but I don't care.

Here's the thing about eavesdropping. You can't exactly say, "I was spying on you and heard what you said, douchebag." On the other hand, they were just standing under the window. It's not like I followed them outside and hid behind the corner to eavesdrop on purpose.

I jump off the bed, go over to the window, and yank the stick out. It slams down in its track with a satisfying *thunk*.

I think I hear Chunk say, "Crap," and I turn out the light and sit with my back against the headboard, waiting for him to come upstairs so I can yell at him and he can apologize.

For everything.

It doesn't happen.

I stare into the dark thinking up all the terrible things I'm going to say to him. Like how he may be smart, but he's an asshole who can't keep a secret and that he's a pig, as bad as Landry in the betrayal department, and that our friendship meant nothing if he'd keep something like being pansexual from me, but tell the rest of the world, and that Brian Candless was right to torment him because he's a piece of shit. Things that will make him cry and say, "I'm sorry, I'm sorry, I'm sorry. I'm so, so sorry."

I wait forever.

I strain my ears, but I don't hear their voices anymore. I don't hear Chunk's tread on the stairs either. He and Annabelle have clearly left the back porch. She's probably giving him kissing tips, or pointers on contraception for his big hookup tomorrow.

There's a rock in my stomach. After a while, the spindles of the headboard feel poky against my back, so I lie down. The word *supine* comes to mind. It was on the verbal portion of the SAT, and I only know it because Chunk once used it in a game of synonyms. So I lie supine, staring up at the ceiling. The rock turns into a gurgling mass, and the bed tilts a little. I breathe in. Breathe out. Eventually I drift off.

Dimly, I'm aware when Chunk comes into the room but by then I'm trying not to be sick. From the beer, from the betrayal, from all of it.

CHAPTER 20

By the time I wake up, the sun is slanting through the window and Chunk isn't in the bed next to mine. My head hurts and my tongue feels like a marching band did their halftime show on it.

I lie there thinking about my traitorous best friend and the fact that he's meeting Lizzy Borden in Riverside today.

And I'm feeling stupid.

Forget whether Chunk sees me as a girl or not. Forget whether or not he's pan. He thinks I'm all about me and *he's not interested in me like THAT.*

So what? I tell myself it makes no difference. He's a free agent, and has every right to meet whatever tart (that word wasn't on the SATs, but I like it, and I have to be fair; *slut* may be too strong a word).

He can meet whatever tart he chooses.

Way to go, Chunk.

I have just closed my eyes again when Annabelle comes

into the room. She must be wearing wooden clogs or something, because her footsteps are *loud*.

"Oh, good! You're up," she says. Even though I try to indicate that no, I am not.

"Chuck and Joe went for a walk on the back acres, but Joe made a quiche before he left. It's in the oven now."

Taciturn Joe plus quiche does not compute, but then these people keep surprising me. I roll over.

"C'mon, we farm people get up early around here," she says. "It's after seven. Chop chop."

"You're not a farm person, you're a premed student," I mumble, my eyes still closed.

She ignores me. "I know you guys need to get on the road as soon as Chuck comes back, and I know he's going to want quiche before he goes. Joe makes the best—you'll die when you smell it—but I have some stuff in my closet I need to get rid of. Come take a look."

I slowly sit up.

"No offense, but you look like you were ridden hard and put away wet," she says.

"How could I be offended at being told I look like a horse?"

"Someone's a little grumpy when she's hungover."

"Are there people who are cheerful about feeling like this?"

I didn't think I was that drunk, but if hangovers occur in proportion to what was consumed, I don't think I ever want to be *really* drunk.

Annabelle waits outside the bathroom while I pee and wash my face.

When I come out she leads me back down the narrow steps and across the kitchen where there is what I am sure is a delicious smell if you're not hungover.

It makes me wonder if my dad had a bachelor party last night. If so, maybe he's feeling the exact same way I'm feeling right now.

— — — — — —

Annabelle pulls me into her room off the kitchen, opens her closet door, and starts pulling out shirts and lightweight jackets and throwing them on the bed. I try not to look greedy, but there's a moss-green jacket with a peplum waist that reminds me a little of a jacket Katharine Hepburn wore in *Adam's Rib* that I think might make my waist look smaller and my hips a little bigger. I want it.

"So I was talking to Chunk last night . . . ," she says.

"I know, I heard."

"He's very protective of you," she says.

"How is it protecting me to lure me to Riverside? He didn't ever tell me *why* we were going there. They probably eat queer people for breakfast there."

"Is the problem that you guys are going there, or is it the *reason* you're going?"

I don't know how to answer that, so I don't.

"How is it protective to blab about me to every random person who comes along?"

Her eyes cloud for a second. "I'm just some random person?"

Even in my crabby haze, I realize I've hurt her feelings.

I pick up an artfully shredded shirt (that I would never wear) and pretend to examine it.

"I just mean there are things he's told people, not just you, about me. Things I thought he'd keep private."

"You didn't hear everything he said," she says.

"I didn't need to."

"It's just . . ."

"Don't tell me," I insist.

"Fine." She sighs theatrically (she's giving me a run for my money in the drama queen department).

"How about this?" she says, pulling a wide leather belt out of her closet. It has little silver filigree circles on it, and it would look great cinching a loose shirt in at the waist. Again, the illusion of a female-shaped body is lovely and beautiful. And even though it's a shitty morning, I feel a little better thinking that I'll be well dressed next fall. No more no-style style.

She hands me a T-shirt that says PRETEND I SAID SOMETHING CLEVER and a black-and-white-checked miniskirt. "Here, try these on," she orders.

I'm suddenly bashful.

"Later," I tell her.

"No! I want to see how they fit before I give them to you."

"Fine." I sigh as theatrically as she did a minute ago. She smiles and steps into the hall.

There's a mirror on the back of the door. It's a little warped, so my torso looks shorter than it is, and my face and legs look longer. The shirt and jacket are cool. The skirt . . . not so much. My legs are white and despite the fact that I've been shaving them for a year now, too masculine looking. Plus my hips are too narrow. I peel it off just as Annabelle knocks.

"Can I see?"

"Just a sec," I call, pulling my jeans back on and opening the door.

She pronounces the combination perfect, and hands me a different skirt and another top.

- - - - - - -

By the time Chunk and Joe get back, I've tried on what feels like fifty different outfits and rejected all but three. My knees just seem too knobby for skirts—even though Annabelle insisted that leggings disguise stuff like that.

Still, the clothing I do choose is fabulous, so at least I have *something* to be grateful for.

CHAPTER 21

It's eight o'clock, we've had breakfast, and it's time to leave. I hug Mamie and shake hands with Joe. Annabelle follows us out to Betty to say goodbye.

I take the Muzzy dress out from my Space Camp duffel and lay it on top of our bags. Sequins don't wrinkle, but I want the fabric underneath to stretch out a little. Annabelle smiles. "I *knew* you had something all picked out."

She and Chunk hug goodbye and even though she says it low, I hear her say, "Just tell her."

Tell me what? I wonder, but then Annabelle releases him and turns to me.

We hug for a long time. I picture Dorothy, near the end of *The Wizard of Oz* when she tells the Scarecrow that she'll miss him most of all. "Keep in touch," Annabelle says, before letting me go.

She stands in front of the house and waves as we drive away.

I have managed not to address Chunk directly once this morning, not even in repacking the car.

He does not seem to care.

We're silent, pulling out of the lane and onto the road that leads back to the highway. I am clenching my teeth so hard that I can almost feel my jaw becoming more square and masculine. Thanks a lot, Chunk.

There's a sign for 80 up ahead.

I can't stand it anymore. "Do you have anything you want to tell me?" I say.

Chunk's eyes don't leave the road. "Like what?" His voice is bored, but I recognize it as the voice he used when someone at school would call him "lard ass" or make some other fat boy comment.

In other words, Fake Bored.

And now he's asking, "Like what?" There's just so much!

Like the fact that he betrayed me by telling his mom I'm trans.

Like the fact that he thinks nothing of trash-talking me to other people, like he did with Annabelle. For some reason, the number one thing that comes out is entirely different.

"Oh, I don't know," I say. "Something about how we're going to be meeting someone in Riverside before we go to Chicago?"

I peer at his face for a reaction, and I have to hand it to him, he's got the Fake Bored thing going on pretty well. It's like he's watching a documentary on mold or something.

Then again, he'd probably be interested in that.

"I figured there was no need to mention it until we got closer," he says in an offhand way.

I adopt the same tone, even though I want to yell. "Would have been nice to know" is all I say.

For what seems like a long time there is only the sound of the road under Betty.

"It wouldn't have been nice for me," he finally says.

"Why not?" I look away. We pull onto the highway, and the accelerated sound almost swallows his next words.

"You would have ruined it."

I look away from the field of cornstalks and back at him. "How would I have ruined it?"

"You would have spent the last two days making fun of me for trying to crash diet before I met her in person, or telling me she was an evil murderer, and I just don't want to hear it."

"But you don't know her! She could be catfishing you! Or an ex-con who's planning to rob us at gunpoint!"

"I *do* know her and she's not. This is exactly why I didn't say anything, Jess. Jesus!"

The Fake Bored is gone and authentic irritation is on his face. It permeates his words, and even though I know

225

he's right, she's probably who she says she is, I can't help myself.

"If we get robbed, you owe me," I spit.

He shakes his head. "All about you," he says, flooring it.

It is 262 very quiet miles from Omaha to Riverside.

CHAPTER 22

It's almost noon, and when we're about five minutes from the turnoff to Riverside, we see a truck parked along the frontage road. In the bed of it, there's a big sign that says STAR TREK FESTIVAL, FUTURE BIRTHPLACE OF CAPTAIN JAMES T. KIRK, 8 MILES.

There's a very one-dimensional hand-painted Starship Enterprise on it.

I don't know what I'd expected, but I suppose I'd pictured something on a grander scale. I look over at Chunk and I can tell by his expression that he did, too. His jaw tightens a little and I can also tell that I'd better not say anything.

We turn off the highway and follow a country road for a few miles. It's actually really pretty; it curves and dips, with fields on either side. Occasionally we pass some farm buildings with towers outside of them that look ridiculously phallic.

We start to see a few houses and then a sign that says WELCOME TO RIVERSIDE. Traffic has increased steadily since we left the highway, and now it's really getting slow. We're behind a Ford Taurus that's covered in bumper stickers. There's the typical BEAM ME UP, SCOTTY. THERE IS NO INTELLIGENT LIFE ON EARTH, but it also has ones that I don't get, like TREKKIE? GET A LIFE, I'M A TREKKER.

Turns out Riverside itself is, oh, two blocks long. You'd think in a town that small parking would be an easy thing, but you would be mistaken. At least today you would be, because there are millions of cars clogging the main street.

Traffic crawls past the museum of the birthplace of Captain Kirk, and there's a replica of the Starship Enterprise on a trailer in the parking lot. The spaceship is not much bigger than, say, a king-size bunk bed.

Chunk turns down a side street. Cars line both sides of the road, and people are walking back toward the middle of town, many of them dressed for the occasion. I see a couple of Klingons, and a Patrick Stewart wannabe. There's an entire family dressed like the original cast. Dad's obviously Captain Kirk, while Mom is in a red dress and a black wig, trying to pull off a white Uhura. The kid in the stroller has pointy Spock ears and is holding what I recognize as a stuffed Tribble, the furry little animal from an episode entitled *The Trouble with Tribbles*. I'm actually surprised at how much the culture of *Star Trek* has seeped into my consciousness without my knowing.

"Where are we going?"

"I'm looking for a place to park," Chunk snaps.

We cruise for a few blocks in silence. There's space on the left, and Chunk makes a tight U-turn to grab it. It is an impressive feat, considering how congested everything is, but I'm in no mood to give out compliments.

He turns off the engine but doesn't get out. Instead he starts texting.

"Okay," he says. "Let's go." I look at the clock on the dash. It's 12:20.

"We have to leave no later than one o'clock," I tell him. We're still a little over three hours from Chicago.

A text *whoosh*es in. Chunk looks at it before getting out of the car.

We lock the doors and start walking in the direction of the downtown.

"Today would be a good day to rob a bank," I say to break the silence. "You could just dress like a Klingon or whatever and then melt into the crowd."

"Do me a favor when you meet her," he says.

"I'm not going to call her Lizzie Borden, or tell her that you've been dieting in anticipation of meeting her!" I snap.

"You're right, you're not," he says in a bossy voice. "I want you to call me Chuck or Christophe when we meet her."

"You hate the name Christophe!" I exclaim.

Chunk stops in the middle of the street. So do I.

He gets right in my face; his eyes are a little wild, like they were when he yelled at Annabelle for making us crash. "You're insane if you think I prefer Chunk to Christophe! Jesus, God Almighty, Jess! What in that twisted, self-absorbed head of yours makes you think anyone in their right mind would like being called Chunk? Especially someone as big as me?"

Shocked, I take a step back. "You never said anything about your nickname."

"I shouldn't have had to. And it wasn't until we met Annabelle that I realized you were still calling me that!"

I think back. It seems incredible that I haven't referred to him by his name in front of him recently, but I can't come up with a single time I would have. It's not like I go around introducing him to people.

"You told your mom about me," I accuse.

"Holy crap, Jess! I ask you not to call me a derogatory nickname and you dismiss it like that? No apology, no 'I'm sorry,' no nothing! You really can't see past your own nose! I have had to listen to you make rude comments about weight forever. *Oooh—it must be bad if this truck is passing our fat ass*," he says in a falsetto that is clearly meant to mimic me. *"Gee, Chunk, you and your mom are so much alike because you're fat!"*

"That's not what I was saying."

But he just goes on. "You're so judgmental—and such an effing hypocrite! You freak out all over the place at the mere thought of people judging you, but you do it all the time!"

"I do not!"

"I *saw* the way you looked at Mamie when we walked in! I know how you look at big people! You make jokes about it all the time!" His voice cracks. "And for the record, yes! I told my mom about you! The night you told me! Did it ever occur to you that it might have been confusing for me, or something I might have needed help understanding?"

A family dressed in *Star Trek* jumpsuits passes us, and he

lowers his voice. "It's not like people are born knowing about gender identity issues. Of course I told her. She's a psychiatrist, for God's sake!"

I suck in my breath. "So you think I'm crazy!"

"That's not what I meant, and you know it."

I start to shake.

"My mom's the one who gave me all the books to help me understand, so I could be a good friend to you! And let me tell you something, it hasn't always been a reciprocal relationship!"

"You're saying I'm a shitty friend?"

"I'm saying there are times when it feels a little one-sided!" Chunk's voice is raised again. "I didn't tell you I was planning to meet up with Lizard because something cool might be happening for *me*, and I can't tell my best friend because she's so effing judgmental!"

"I am not!"

"Oh, you met her online?" he says, again with the falsetto. *"She can't be a cool person; she has to be a serial killer because who else would be interested in my fat friend?"* His eyes well up.

"That's not what I think! It's just you've never—" I was going to say *met her*, but Chunk jumps in.

"Had someone interested in me? I know! And now you think it's fake because it's not in person."

"You talked shit about me to Annabelle," I accuse, determined to get this fight back to where it should be—focused on the way he lied to me, outed me to his mom, and how he lied to me about why he wanted to come to Riverside.

"Again with the deflection and trying to turn it back into how poor Jess has been so abused! You're making my point for me!"

A couple of kids on skateboards shoot by us. The backs of my eyes feel pinched together.

"If that's really how you feel, why did you bother convincing me to go on this trip with you?"

He studies me for a minute, his gaze as unfriendly as I've ever seen it. "I'm asking myself that very question."

"Oh, wait, I know," I say, my voice nastier than my mom's, back before she found inner peace. "So you could dupe me into going to some shithole town in Iowa to get some action with your Internet girlfriend!"

"You think I needed you for that?" he shouts, and I notice the people around us are giving us wide berth. "For your information, I had no idea Riverside even existed until two nights ago. I had no intention of meeting Lizard until then! So this was never a plan about me, because it never is!"

"You only got obsessed with Lizard two nights ago when we left Tahoe? Why?"

His face is red, but the question stops him for a second.

"I'm not obsessed!" is what he finally comes out with. He's quiet for a minute. We stare at each other. And when he speaks again it's in his more logical, normal, calm Chunk way.

"Look, the original plan was to get you to open your eyes to the fact that your dad might have not signed the waiver because he didn't understand what's really going on with you. But that doesn't make him a transphobe, just an ignorant person! Also you've only heard one side of the story for the last two years, and it might be a good thing—a healthy thing—for you to hear your dad's version of what happened with him and your mom and Jan!" Chunk takes a deep breath. "I also had this stupid effing idea that it would be fun to take a road trip with my best friend. And even though I've known Lizard for a year, none of my originally wanting to take this trip had a damn thing to do with her."

Once he mentions my dad I barely hear anything else he says. So now he's siding with my dad. Seriously?

"I'll wait in the car while you get it on with Lizard," I say, spinning on my heel and heading back toward Betty.

"I'm not . . . whatever, Jess. You don't even have the keys," he says to my back.

Without turning around I fish in my pocket, pull out the spare, and hold it up so he can see it.

I keep walking.

He doesn't follow me.

CHAPTER 23

It's hot and muggy in the car, even with the windows down.
After a half hour of ruminating and stewing, I get out and
walk in the opposite direction of town.

The physical exercise heats me up even more.

He called me judgmental! What an asshole! And was he
siding with my dad?

The road slopes upward and I charge ahead.

Still, those other things he said . . . I honestly never knew
it bothered him that I thought of him as Chunk, or that he
thought I was thinking of him as a fat guy. I do make comments about other people's looks. And I have called Jan a fat
cow since she stole my dad. But that was just an insult, something I knew would hurt her to hear, even if I never said it in
front of her. It didn't occur to me until just this second that
what I said about Jan would hurt Chunk's feelings.

He's just Chunk. Chuck. Christophe. Whatever he wants
to be called. I think when you know someone for a long time,
you don't think about what they look like, you think about

what they are. I see him as my best friend, inventor of games, personal sounding board, and I love that, because even though I bitch about the way he always wants to talk about my feelings, it secretly feels good that someone cares.

Not just someone.

Him.

When I look at him, I see his intelligent eyes, his goofy expressions, his steady regard . . . his halo of black hair, the dimple in his cheek. I see . . .

I see the person I love most in the world.

Everything freezes with that thought.

Chunk is the person I love most in the world. LOVE love. Even if he doesn't love me back *that* way. Even if he can't love me back *that* way. All of my weird jealousy about Lizard slides into focus . . . and oh, crap.

I hurt the feelings of the person I love most in the world.

I hurt Chunk's feelings.

I hurt Chuck.

And no wonder he went dashing into the (virtual) arms of Lizard.

I turn around and start running toward town. Maybe if I apologize, maybe if I promise to be better, maybe if I . . .

I don't finish the thought, because just as I get to the car, I see *Chun— Chuck* walking toward it. And he's not alone. He's with a girl who's wearing a tight little Uhura dress. She has purple hair, an eyebrow piercing, and gauges in her ears. She's rail thin, and I can't help but notice, even from this distance, that the dress is poorly constructed. The hem is way crooked and one sleeve is noticeably wider than the other. It looks like a six-year-old sewed it. But that's me, being judgmental. *I will be nice, I will be nice, I will be nice.*

Chuck and Lizard (because obviously that's who it is) are laughing and talking like they know each other. *I will be nice.*

Chuck looks over and sees me. He breaks off mid-laugh.

"Hey," I call out, heading toward them. He doesn't call hey back. We meet by Betty.

"Lizard, right?" I ask, to show him I am not calling her Lizzie Borden.

"Lizard or Elizabeth," she tells me in a friendly way.

"Chuck's told me a lot about you," I say, to show him I have taken to heart his desire not to be called Chunk.

Lizard nods and smiles. "He's told me a lot about you too, Jess."

She has a slight lisp because her tongue is pierced. Or maybe it's just a bit of a speech defect.

Either way, I am not judging.

Chuck doesn't say anything. Instead he opens the back hatch and grabs his Space Camp bag. *What's he doing?*

"Hey, it's almost one o'clock," I tell him.

He grabs his laptop case too, then slams the hatch.

"Actually, I'm going to stick around here for a while," he says, not looking at me. "Lizard lives in Chicago. She'll give me a ride into the city later."

I look at Lizard, who smiles an uncomfortable smile.

"But my dad's wedding," I say stupidly.

Even though I've never had a solid plan, every nonplan I did have involved Chuck at my side. Either helping me throw my dad's mail in his face, or magnanimously forgiving Jan.

None of my plans *didn't* involve Chuck. My brain can't process the idea of him not being there.

"You can tell me all about it after," he says in an offhand tone.

"Yeah, we'll see you then. Chuck said the wedding's at St. Lucy's. I know right where that is," Lizard says a little too cheerfully. I can tell she knows this is not okay with me.

"Fine," I say, stalking around Betty and getting into the driver's side. "If I have time after the wedding, I'll help you fix your costume."

Of course I won't. But I want her to know how shitty she looks.

CHAPTER 24

Numb, I follow I-80 until the gently rolling hills of Iowa become the flat lines of Illinois. My eyes are dried husks. There are no tears left to cry, and the anxiety in my belly has been replaced with a dead white space.

The sun is high in the sky, and if I didn't know from the occasional highway sign that I'm driving east, I would have no idea what direction I'm going. The low plane of the landscape out here is disorienting.

I am in love with someone who has abandoned me for a girl who was born that way.

I am in love with someone who can't stand me because I am selfish and judgmental and a hypocrite.

And now I am heading to the wedding of a man who probably does not even want me there because I will be an embarrassment to him.

If I had a Delete button for the last three days, I'd press it.

Traffic thickens, telling me we're approaching the city, but up ahead just looks like a big town at first. You'd think the first thing I saw would be the skyscrapers.

Betty's oil light goes on and I want to scream. And then I do.

I am on Interstate 80, approaching my father's wedding, and I am screaming.

This is what a nervous breakdown looks like, I think.

I scream it out. I scream at Betty for being a shitty car and having an oil leak. I scream rage at my dad for refusing to see the truth of who I am and for not allowing me to do something about it sooner. I scream rage at him for his leaving my mom and me, at Jan for snaking in and stealing him. I scream at Chuck for not loving me, at myself for thinking Chuck could ever love me the way I want him to, at the universe for giving me a penis instead of a vagina.

I scream until my throat is raw and I realize there are other cars on the road, passing me.

I gradually stop screaming. The oil light is still on. Of course.

I start looking for a gas station.

My brain is scattered, spent, empty, but a single thought remains: *Do not ruin Betty.* By the time I see a sign that says sixteen miles to Chicago, I'm hollow.

Up ahead there's a Kwik Trip gas station sitting next to a Subway sandwich shop. I turn off 80, and pull into the station.

I grab my dress. It's after four, but I'll bet the people getting married have to show up at the church early, and I want my dad's first sight of me to be me in the dress. I'll change in the bathroom after I buy oil.

I snag my Space Camp bag from the back and dig into it for my wallet. And SHIT!!! This is not my Space Camp bag. It's Chuck's.

Which means he has mine.

And my wallet.

I almost start screaming again.

Shit.

Shit.

Shit.

How am I going to buy oil?

I leave the imposter Space Camp bag where it is and carry my dress and backpack to the front of the car. I lay the dress on the hood and then dump my backpack onto the driver's seat and start digging around in it, hoping a stray five might have fallen out somewhere. Underneath my album there's the cache of mail, including the yellow envelope that arrived on my birthday and the red one that arrived on Christmas. I pray to a god I don't necessarily believe in that there is money inside one of them, and that the money is not in the form of a check.

I tear open the birthday card, and am rewarded by the sight of green currency. I pull it out, put the card on the dashboard, and count five crisp twenties. I shake my head at my dad's trust in the postal system. Lucky me, though.

I grab the money and the dress, and go inside to buy oil. The clerk barely looks up from the register when she hands me the change.

I lock myself in the women's restroom, hang the dress on

the nozzle for the hand dryer, and put the ballet flats next to it on the floor.

The dress feels heavier than I remember when I slide it over my head. It has a side zipper that scratches the skin under my arm. I tug it away from my body a little.

There's no mirror in here, but it feels a little tighter in the hips than it was just a few weeks ago. Still, the tightness and the weight of it make me feel . . . glamorous somehow.

Stomach thrumming, I grab my other clothes and step out of the restroom. The clerk doesn't laugh. But she doesn't applaud either. She doesn't seem to notice me at all.

I grab a paper funnel and go out to add the oil, feeling expert. Annabelle would be proud.

Before I start Betty up, I glance down at the card.

I can't throw this one at him now, because he'll see I opened it.

I look it over before throwing it away. It's yellow to match the envelope and has a generic looking cake on it.

He gets two points for gender neutrality at least.

I open it and a note falls out. The handwriting on the card itself is Jan's.

Dear Jeremy,
We miss you.
Love, Dad and Jan

I'm not sure about that.

It feels weird that she signed the card for both of them, and my feelings are hurt a little on my mom's behalf.

And mine.

I open the note to see my dad's scrawl.

Dear Jeremy,

Happy Birthday.

I don't know if you'll ever read this, or if you throw away mail from me as soon as it arrives, but it almost doesn't matter. I'm writing to you for me. And I'll say the same thing I say in every letter so that if you do open one, you'll read what I'm saying, and if on the odd chance you do read each one, my words will be emphasized.

I love you.

I can't tell you how much I miss you, or how much I wish things were different between us. You told me that your feelings about yourself have nothing to do with me, but I worry they do. A huge part of me regrets moving out when your mom asked me to, thinks that if I'd insisted on staying in the house for the sake of raising you, things might have been different. Or if I'd at least not moved to Chicago when I did.

It's too late to reverse any of those things now but I want you to know, those are things I think about every single day. Just as I think about you every day. And love you.

Dad

My mom *asked* my dad to leave? No one ever told me the details.

I just came home from Chuck's that day to find Dad's closet empty and his car gone. She said they were getting divorced, and that was it.

No more discussion.

During the last fight they had, when he threatened to put her out of the car, I could tell he'd had it. And then when I caught Jan at his house and thought back to the meaningful glance between them . . .

God, I feel stupid for assuming things that weren't true.

I pull Betty to the side of the gas station and grab my phone. Even as I'm clicking on MOMSTER in the contacts, I realize I'm not calling just to get the scoop.

I'm in love with my best friend and he's ditched me and I'm miserable and I want my mom.

But when she answers, I can't say that.

"Did you throw Dad out?" I ask when she picks up on the third ring.

"Well, hello, Jess. It's nice to hear from you!"

I repeat myself and there's a pause. I rub the steering wheel with my thumb.

"Is everything okay, honey?"

Her tenderness is a relief; a gate opens, and tears I didn't know I had left slide down my face. Everything is *not* okay.

"Sweetie?" She sounds worried.

"Chuck's not coming to Dad's wedding and I'm driving alone to Chicago." I hate it that I'm crying, now sobbing audibly, but I can't help it. "He stayed behind in Riverside."

"He *what*?"

"He likes another girl and he met up with her there and he stayed behind."

"That little shit!" Her voice is so loud my body jerks. "Just like that? He left you to drive all by yourself? Do you want me to fly you home after the wedding?" she asks, and before I can even really consider it, she lets loose. "Let him drive back on his own! I hope his car breaks down!"

I'm so surprised, the tears stop immediately.

"Mom?"

"I mean it! What kind of a jerk abandons his best friend on a cross-country trip? As soon as we get off the phone, I'm calling his mother!"

I cringe. It's not like we're in third grade. "Mom, wait. He's supposed to catch a ride into Chicago later. Let me talk to him before you call Dr. Kefala."

She's quiet, and then I hear her breathing in a rhythm I recognize as her centering-myself breath work.

Breathe in, 2, 3, 4; breathe out, 5, 6, 7, 8, 9.

"I'm sorry," she says after a few cycles. Zen Mary is back. "Having your mom fly off the handle when you're hurting isn't too helpful, is it?"

Through the windshield I see little blackbirds lined up on the gas station sign.

"I wouldn't say it isn't . . . even if it doesn't seem to follow Spiritual Forgiveness," I tell her.

"Spiritual Forgiveness definitely takes a hike when someone hurts your child," she acknowledges. "But sometimes you just need to honor the feeling and let it pass."

I'm glad she can't see me, because I have to roll my eyes at that.

"Nobody ever told me exactly what happened. I always thought Dad left us."

She doesn't hesitate at the subject switch. "I'm sorry." Her voice is sympathetic. "I didn't realize that's what you thought. I did ask him to leave, but he was only too willing to go. The single thing we ever agreed on was that our fighting was bad for you. Does it matter?"

A car door slams and the blackbirds take off.

"I guess not. I just kind of always thought you maybe felt abandoned." I don't want to bring up Jan. "And sometimes I worried that it left you lonely."

"What makes you think I'm lonely?"

"I don't know." I feel bad saying it, like it's going to seem as though I think she's pathetic. "You always want to do stuff together, and you keep saying you miss me and . . . you said you were afraid I was missing them when I came out to you."

"Did I?" she asks.

"Yes."

"I don't remember—but I suppose that was at a time when I thought I hated them. It must have been jealousy. Not loneliness, though."

I let that sink in.

"I'm so sorry you've been carrying this around with you. I feel like a bad mother."

"You're not a bad mother," I tell her.

"You're not a bad daughter," she says.

I glance down at the clock. It's five after four.

"I'd better get going."

"Yes, you'd better! Give me a call when you know what's happening with Chuck."

"I will."

"Bye-bye, honey. I love you more than anything."

Just as I say, "I love you, too," she says, "But not in a lonely creepy-mom way."

I smile for a second after we hang up.

Chuck was right when he corrected me for assuming Jan had something to do with my dad leaving us.

As soon as I have the thought, I shut it down. I can't think about it right now. I can't think of him at all.

I pull back out onto the road, determined to focus on something else. Which turns out to be the blue Ford sedan directly in front of me.

Until it gets off on one of the exits.

Then I focus on the red Chevy truck that had previously been in front of the blue Ford.

But Chuck creeps in again.

He should be with me right now.

Red truck. Red truck. Red truck.

He's supposed to be by my side. He's supposed to back me up when I tell my dad to accept me as I am, or never see me again.

Red truck. Think about the red truck ahead.

I follow behind it for twenty minutes or so.

"Exit to Smith Road, one and a half miles ahead on your right," says the disembodied voice of the GPS.

Something oozes in my stomach. I imagine thickened paint coating my insides, then pooling in the middle.

This is it.

I follow directions to the off-ramp, down two blocks, and into the almost empty parking lot of St. Lucy's.

Despite Chicago traffic's best effort to make me late, I'm an hour and fifteen minutes early.

There are just two other cars there, a white van that says Flowers by Flora (which is the kind of redundant name that I believe to be responsible for the death of small businesses) and a black limousine that tells me at least Jan must be here.

What if my dad hasn't arrived yet? I park Betty near the exit, facing out, just in case I need to get away fast.

Paint-stomach churning, I make my way across the parking lot.

My back is damp. *Humid*, I think. I used to mix that word up with human. I remember telling my second-grade teacher I was a humid being. My back is wet, so I guess it's true.

The front steps are steep, and hard to navigate gracefully. I flash on a vision of leaning on Chuck's arm.

Get through this first before thinking about Chuck.

I step through massive oak doors into a church that's empty except for a woman kneeling in the aisle, attaching heather-colored ribbons to the ends of the pews.

"Excuse me?" She looks up. "Do you know if the groom is here yet?"

She nods, pointing toward an arched opening near the front of the chapel. "Bride's that way." She points to one on the opposite side of the altar. "Groom's that way. You family?"

I nod.

"Congratulations," she says.

"Thanks," I mumble, heading for the groom's side. The church didn't look that big from the outside, but the aisle feels like it is the longest one in the world.

The arch leads into a little hallway. One of the doors leading off it has a hand-lettered sign that says RESERVED FOR THE GROOM.

I'm standing in front of it, my tongue thick, when the door at the end of the hallway opens and sunlight streams in. Someone—it must be Flora the Florist—bustles in with an armload of flowers. I step aside so she can pass into the chapel, and she smiles at me.

"Don't you look pretty!" she exclaims over her shoulder.

And in that moment, on this day of revelations, I'm slammed with the awareness of yet another important thing.

I realize how badly I want my father to say the same thing the florist did.

I want him to hug me, and tell me I'm beautiful, and call me his daughter.

I want him to see that my gender identity has absolutely nothing to do with him.

I want him to think I'm okay—even better than okay.

My mouth is dry and icy at the same time. Like the Atacama desert.

Because I know he doesn't, and he won't ever.

You assume that, but you haven't talked to your dad in over a year. How do you know he hasn't changed his mind? I hear Chuck's voice in my head.

I force my hand to knock.

Too soft. The florist is coming back through, empty-handed. She's going to think I'm a freak, just standing here. *His letter said he wished things were different and he missed me.*

I knock harder.

"Come in," my dad calls. I grit my teeth and open the door.

He's alone in the room, standing in front of an old fashioned full-length oval mirror. His attention is on the bow tie he's attempting to tie, and it's immediately obvious he's having trouble. One side is way too long.

His hazel eyes meet mine in the mirror, take in the top part of the Muzzy dress.

There's a split second to see shock in his reflection before he spins around to face me.

"Jeremy?"

Is that panic on his face?

"What are you doing here?"

My mouth goes from icy to hot coal. I forget all about the words in his letter.

I want to yell, *I knew you didn't want me here!* Instead, I say very quietly, "I came for the wedding. I don't have to stay."

He takes a step forward. "No! I just . . . you made it clear you weren't coming."

"Right."

"Really, I'm just surprised!" He steps in and gives me an awkward hug.

It is like being hugged by a life-size Lego person.

After a brief torture, we both take a step back.

"So, uh, how did you get here?"

The hot coal slides into my stomach.

"Look, Dad, I can just leave."

"No! I'm really happy you're here. I'm just . . . processing."

He's staring at me. The bow tie dangles in his right hand and I feel naked. Alien. A specimen from another planet.

"Is your mom in Chicago, too?"

"No, I came with Chun— Chuck."

He nods, no doubt relieved. He hasn't seen the (mostly) mellow New Age hippie version of Mom.

We stare at each other.

His hair is thinner on top than it was the last time I saw him—nothing approaching a comb-over, but I can definitely see scalp. His shoulders aren't as broad as I remember either.

Our stare-off lasts and lasts.

"You look so different" is what he finally comes up with.

"Hormones," I say, not caring that it comes out like a taunt. His Adam's apple bobs and he gestures toward me with the non–bow tie hand.

"Is this . . . Is this how you dress now?"

What are you doing here, how did you get here, and is this how you dress?

"Forget it. Coming was a bad idea," I mutter, turning back toward the door.

I left the cards in the car. Do I go back out and get them and then come back to throw them at him or what?

He stops me with a hand on my elbow.

"I didn't mean . . . it's just, I'm not used to it."

I shake it off.

"This *isn't* how I dress all the time. It's just how I dress to go to a wedding!" For a minute I feel stupid in my outfit. "It's not like you wear a bow tie every day."

He nods like he gets it.

"If it makes you happy to dress this way, then . . ."

I cut him off.

"It's not about the clothes! It's never been about the clothes, Dad. You don't get it."

Tears bud in my eyes. It's not like transgender people haven't been all over the news. He's had plenty of time to educate himself, and clearly he hasn't.

"You still don't understand!"

My dad raises his voice. "Then help me understand!"

I raise mine to match his. "It's not my job to educate you!"

The tips of his ears turn red.

"Listen, mister! You don't get to have it both ways. You can't just show up here, tell me I don't understand, refuse to help me understand, and then bitch that I don't get you." His voice catches.

"But you don't! You think it's just a phase!"

"How do you know it isn't?"

That stops me.

How do I know?

I know it the way I know the color of my eyes. I know it the way I know if I stop taking hormones, my hair will eventually recede like his. I know it in the cells of my body,

I know it the way I know we're all just matter, made up of carbon and oxygen and mostly water.

Just as I know he is never going to call me his daughter.

I turn for the door again.

"Damn it, Jeremy!" he explodes. "You don't get to waltz in here an hour before I'm getting married and pick a fight with me!"

"I knew you didn't want your freak trans daughter here!" I choke out.

His voice is low. "I wanted you here."

"The real me, or the me you want me to be?"

"I want my child to have an easier life than the one you're choosing."

Before I can react to the word *choosing* he grabs me in a hug. It's tight, nothing like the awkward Lego one.

"I love you. I don't understand you, and you won't explain, but I love you."

In this muddle of a hug, I feel him shaking.

He's crying.

And my heart, mangled and raw from the last two days— from the last two years—shreds even further.

Because what do you do with that?

He doesn't see me for who I am, but he loves me. And both things feel important, but really hard to reconcile.

My arms come up to hug him back.

CHAPTER 25

The ceremony is . . . ceremony like.

Before it started, I got my album from the car and went to see Jan. She hugged me and cried, and then introduced me to Eliza, her maid of honor, as my father's child, an amazing artist. I appreciated the gender neutrality of the introduction.

Eliza left to give us some privacy, but art school and my portfolio and her job at the museum were all we talked about.

There was just too much other stuff to say right then.

It was kind of a relief when Eliza came back to tell us the ceremony needed to start soon, and I left to take my seat.

In a weird way, I felt bad that Jan had a maid of honor who wasn't my mom . . . even though that would have been incredibly freaky.

— — — — —

Now I'm sitting in the back of the church rather than up front where my dad and Jan wanted me to. Stupid, but

I had a teeny hope that Chuck would come at the last minute.

Of course, he doesn't.

I try not to think about what he's doing right now, and I focus on the minister, who's droning on in some ministerial way. He's reading something about a gazelle leaping. Or maybe it's just a heart leaping like a gazelle. I can't quite connect my father with the image. Who picks the readings for this kind of thing? Like, did my dad and Jan sit down together and choose this particular one? *Oh, that's us, you are the leaping gazelle and I am your fair love.*

I study their backs. Jan's wearing heels, and she's taller than my dad in them. He's not *Wizard of Oz* Lollipop-Guild short, but he looks even shorter than I remember him being, or maybe it's just that the ceiling of the church is so high.

Jan's wearing a plainish beige dress with an eyelet hem. It's understated and perfect. She isn't a size 6, or even a size 14, but when she reaches over and takes my dad's hand, I have to admit that doesn't matter.

Which is a pretty dumb and late observation for someone who's trans to make . . . but Chunk—*Chuck*—was right.

It's never occurred to me that I'm not the only one who sees myself differently from the way other people do. That other people struggle with image and self-image in different ways. There is Chuck and his weight; Annabelle and her cigarette smoking, magenta-haired self, hiding the fact that she's a premed nerd.

Does it make the way we see ourselves any less valid if other people don't share our vision?

I decide it doesn't.

－ － － － －

When the minister pronounces Dad and Jan husband and wife, they turn to kiss each other and it feels weird. Not bad, just weird. Like it's the end of an era. And even though that era was a really wretched one with a lot of fighting in it, and I would never want it back, it was the era of me, my mom, and my dad as a family.

Before the music starts for them to come back down the aisle, I slip out the door to go sit in Betty, hoping against hope that Chunk, *Chuck*, is out there.

Of course, he isn't.

My dad told me before the ceremony that he wants me to ride to the reception with him and Jan in the limo, but I told them I was going to wait for Chuck and then we'd come together.

I don't know if that's true.

I have no idea what to do. Do I text him with the address of the reception and tell him I'll meet him there? Do I just wait here for a few hours until he comes? Even if he's hooking up with Lizard, he has to meet me at some point, right? I have his car. The thought that he could be hooking up with Lizard churns my stomach. Should I take my mom up on her offer to fly me home?

The doors open and people start coming out of the church and milling around. There's a tall guy who kind of looks like an older male version of Jan, and he's going around shaking people's hands. The crowd parts and my dad and Jan step out of the doors. I see them looking around.

For me?

People blow soap bubbles. I watch as a little kid in a blue short suit spills his. He looks like he's about to cry until his mom leans down and holds her container and wand so he can blow. For some reason my throat tightens.

People crowd around Dad and Jan, and I can see my dad, craning his neck this way and that. He *is* looking for me.

I check my lipstick in the rearview mirror and then get out of Betty.

My dad sees me right away.

"Come here!" he calls, beckoning with one arm, the other firmly planted around Jan. They're both glowing, but is it my imagination or do they both glow brighter with my approach?

"This is my kid," my dad says, to everyone. "Jess."

And hearing him speak my chosen name keeps me smiling the entire time the three of us pose for pictures.

— — — — — —

Eventually the limo pulls up in front of the church.

"You have the address, right?" Jan checks.

I nod.

"Come as soon as he gets here," my dad instructs.

"I will," I say, wondering if I'm telling the truth.

Once my dad and Jan are gone, I cross the parking lot again, and stand next to Betty.

What should I do?

People are getting into their cars around me, and a small blond girl blows bubbles all the way to hers. The bubbles sail lazily in the air until they hit the sides of the church and pop. One makes it up and over the edge of the building.

When the last car leaves the parking lot and I'm about to get back into Betty, a little gray Toyota pulls in off the street and heads straight toward me.

Chuck gets out, leans in to grab his bags, and then clumsily hugs the driver. Who is Lizard, of course.

She beeps her horn twice, waves, and drives off. Chuck walks toward me, and then stops several feet away.

I am so happy to see him—and so happy there was no long, passionate goodbye kiss with Lizard—that I burst into tears.

He takes a hesitant step toward me, sees me crying, and stops again.

"I'm sorry," I blubber. "I'm sorry, I'm sorry, I'm sorry."

I am. For everything.

For the thoughtless fat comments over the years. For not realizing he was actually being bullied by Brian Candless. For not asking him how *he* feels. For being a shitty friend. For not thanking him for being a good one. For endlessly talking about myself and my dissatisfaction with my body, and never even considering that he might be dissatisfied with the way he fits into the envelope of his body.

I'm sorry I've never told him that his body is perfect to

me because it holds the entity that is Christophe David Kefala. But that if he needed to change it, I'd love it then too.

"I'm an asshole," I hiccup.

He steps closer. "Me too," he says.

"I missed your dad's wedding." He looks back toward the church. "I just . . . I got freaked out."

He's still not looking at me.

"By the wedding?"

"No, by you."

And there it is.

"The freaky trans girl," I say.

He looks directly at me. "You don't understand."

My nose is running.

"I'm not freaked out by your transition. Once I understood it, it made perfect sense to me." He starts talking really fast, like he needs to get it over with quickly.

This is not the Chuck I'm used to seeing.

"I'm freaked out by my reaction to you. People aren't supposed to think about their best friends the way I think about you. Especially not when their best friends are going through something huge. I told Annabelle everything last night and she wanted me to tell you—but I didn't because even if it were okay for me to think about you that way, I know you think I'm a disgusting fat slob."

"I don't! I never did!"

He continues talking, still fast, like he didn't hear me.

"Mrs. Harris thinking we were a couple really tortured me. Because I knew you were going to make fun of it. And then Lizard got in touch, and I made this whole plan to come visit her, because I thought the only way to keep our friendship was to quit thinking of you like that. And the only way I could think to make that happen was to see if I could get interested in someone else."

When Chuck stops talking he has a horrified look on his face, like he can't believe what he just said.

And what he just said takes a minute to sink in.

"And did you get interested in her?"

My knees are weak.

He looks at the ground. "She's great." A tangerine-sized lump forms in my throat. "But she's not you."

Before I can stop myself, I fling my body toward his, grab his shoulders, and kiss him. His lips are almost rigid at first, but then they soften and he's kissing me back.

There we are, standing in a deserted church parking lot in Chicago, kissing like crazy, and I never want to stop.

Dad, Mom, Jan, body image, passing, not passing, fly away.

I'm crying again, my lips still pressed against his, but now the tears are from relief and recognition.

There is no Black Hole, just infinity.

ACKNOWLEDGMENTS

Before I was a writer, I thought acknowledgments at the end of a book were a waste of time and paper. This was before I had a front-row seat to the production of making a book and getting it out into the world. With that said, the following is a list of individuals I'd like to thank. I apologize in advance for the length. (Hey, I have a grateful heart!)

To Joy Peskin—I believe my dedication page says it all. You don't get a mention here too. Okay. You do. You deserve it. Thank you, Tracey Adams, as always, for your fabulous literary matchmaking, and for "getting" me. (Were you a psychology major, perchance?)

Heartfelt thanks to the whole FSG BFYR team, with special thanks to Angie Chen, fabulous assistant editor; Anne Diebel, senior creative director; and Katie Cicatelli-Kuc, sharp-eyed production editor. Thanks to Elizabeth Clark, for an absolutely amazing cover, and also to copy editor extraordinaire Maya Packard. (This is where I point out that any mistakes are my own, and she nods her head yes. ☺) Thank you, Brielle Benton, for your hard work in trade marketing, and an especially special thanky thanks to Katie Halata, for doing what you do to get my books into schools and libraries. (I realized while I was typing that you've done this for all four of my books, which means that except for my relationship with my agent, our lit relationship is my longest-standing one. This makes me happy!)

Huge gratitude goes to my amazing kids. I treasure your support, insight, and shenanigans. Thank you, Jeanne Clark, for many things, such as giving birth to me, but also for helping me figure out the answer to a medical question in this book. A gigantic thank-you to Russell Parker, for many, many things, plus an amazing road trip. Who knew research could be so much fun? Thank you, Kathleen Wolski and Kevin McCaughey, for coming to my rescue in the tenth hour, and Jim Averbeck, for swooping in with resources and frolicking at the eleventh. Thank you to Marina Lighthouse, and also to Dr. Harun "Ron" Evcimen, for support, information, and input. Thank you, Jackie Lynde, Alex Lynn Haertjens, and Michael Plondaya, for an amazing afternoon of conversation about . . . stuff, and for being your own sweet selves. I'm grateful to the Book Passage gang, especially Katherine Ralph, for enlightening conversations about moms and kids, Cheryl McKeon, for amazing ninja scheduling and support, and Cary Heater, for keeping this book out of the bay. Thank you to Joanne Pappas Nottage and the Kawika's Ocean Beach Deli crew, along with my Shut Up and Write! comrades, who meet there on

Wednesdays at 5 p.m. (If you're in the area, stop by!) Thank you to Julie Lindow, Donna Brodman, and Peter Maravelis, for cheering me on so, and for providing me with entertaining incentives to sit down and write. A loving thank-you to Kara Lynn Esborg, for your fabulous energy. A shimmery, shining thank-you to my Heavenly Essence Qigong siblings (especially to Madame Doctor Em Segmen). *Zheng qi* to you all.

And finally, a sincere and grateful thank-you to all of my readers, especially the ones who've shared their struggles and triumphs with me.

You inspire me every day.